FREE STUFF FOR KIDS

Our Pledge

We have collected and examined the best free and up-to-a-dollar offers that we could find (plus a few extra-special over-a-dollar values!). Each supplier in this book has promised to honor properly made requests for **single items** through **1993.** Though mistakes do happen, we are doing our best to make sure this book really works.

Distributed by Simon & Schuster
New York

The Free Stuff Editors

Director: Bruce Lansky
Editor: Elizabeth H. Weiss
Researcher: Carla Foley
Editorial Coordinator: Jay Johnson

Designer: Tabor Harlow
Desktop Coordinator: Jon C. Wright
Production Coordinator: Matthew Thurber

ISBN: 0-88166-191-0
Simon & Schuster Ordering #: 0-671-79206-7

ISSN: 1056-9693
16th edition

Published by Meadowbrook Press, 18318 Minnetonka Boulevard, Deephaven, MN 55391.

BOOK TRADE DISTRIBUTION by Simon & Schuster, a division of Simon and Schuster, Inc., 1230 Avenue of the Americas, New York, NY 10020.

92 93 5 4 3 2 1

Printed in the United States of America

Contents

Thank You's

To Pat Blakely, Barbara Haislet, and Judith Hentges for creating and publishing the original *Rainbow Book*, and for proving that kids, parents, and teachers would respond enthusiastically to a source of free things by mail. They taught us the importance of carefully checking the quality of each item and doing our best to make sure that each and every request is satisfied.

Our heartfelt appreciation goes to hundreds of organizations and individuals for making this book possible. The suppliers and editors of this book have a common goal: to make it possible for kids to reach out and discover the world by themselves.

USING THIS BOOK

About This Book

Free Stuff for Kids contains listings of hundreds of items to send away for. The Free Stuff Editors have examined every item and think they're among the best offers available. There are no trick offers—only safe, fun, and informative things you'll like!

This book is designed for kids who can read and write. The directions in **Using This Book** explain exactly how to request an item. Read the instructions carefully so you know how to send a request. Making sure you've filled out a request correctly is easy—just complete the ***Free Stuff for Kids* Checklist** on p. 8. Half the fun is using the book on your own. The other half is getting a real reward for your efforts!

Each year the Free Stuff Editors create a new edition of this book, taking out old items, inserting new ones, and changing addresses and prices. It is important for you to use an updated edition because the suppliers honor properly made requests for single items for the **current** edition only. If you use this edition after **1993,** your request might not be honored.

Getting Your Book in Shape

Before sending for free stuff, get your book in shape. Fold it open one page at a time, working from the two ends toward the middle. This will make the book lie flat when you read or copy addresses.

Reading Carefully

Read the descriptions of the offers carefully to find out exactly what you're getting. Here are some guidelines to help you know what you're sending for:

- A pamphlet or foldout is usually one sheet of paper folded over and printed on both sides.
- A booklet is usually larger and contains more pages, but it's smaller than a book.

Following Directions

It's important to follow each supplier's directions. On one offer, you might need to use a postcard. On another offer, you might be asked to include money or a long self-addressed, stamped envelope. If you do not follow the directions **exactly,** you might not get your request. Ask for only **one** of anything you send for. Family or classroom members using the same book must send separate requests.

Sending Postcards

A postcard is a small card you can write on and send through the mail without an envelope. Many suppliers offering free items require you to send requests on postcards. Please do this. It saves them the time it takes to open many envelopes.

The post office sells postcards with pre-printed postage. The cost of these postcards is 19¢. You can also buy postcards at a drugstore and put stamps on them yourself. (Postcards with a picture on them are usually more expensive.) You must use a postcard that is at least 3 ½ by 5 ½ inches. (The post office will not take 3-by-5-inch index cards.) Your postcards should be addressed like the one below.

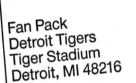

Jessie Rogers
2415 Lake Street
Solon Springs, WI 54873

Fan Pack
Detroit Tigers
Tiger Stadium
Detroit, MI 48216

Dear Sir or Madam:

Please send me a Detroit Tigers fan pack.

Thank you very much.

Sincerely yours,
Jessie Rogers

2415 Lake Street
Solon Springs, WI 54873

- **Neatly print** the supplier's address on the side of the postcard that has the postage. Put your return address in the upper left-hand corner of that side as well.
- **Neatly print** your request, your name, and your address on the blank side of the postcard.
- Do not abbreviate the name of your street or city.
- Use a ballpoint pen.

Sending Letters

Your letters should look like the one below.

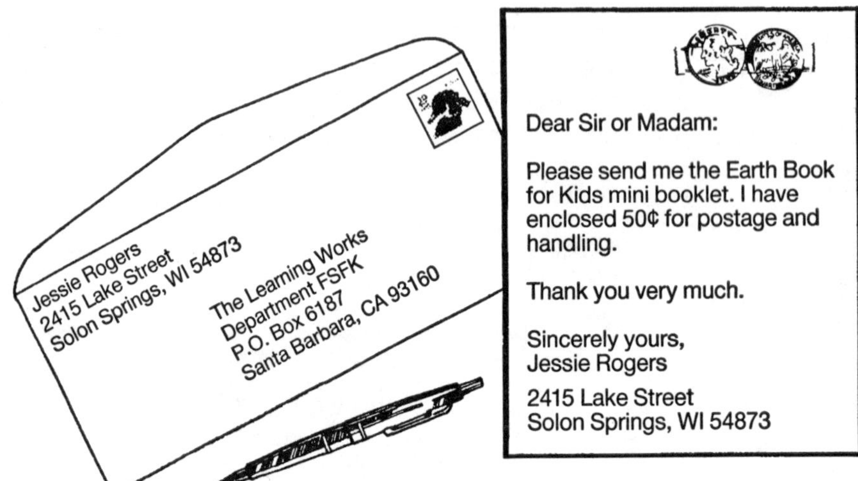

- **Neatly print** the name of the item you want exactly as you see it in the directions.
- **Neatly print** your own name and address at the bottom of the letter. (Do not abbreviate the name of your street or city.)
- If you're including coins or a long self-addressed, stamped envelope, say so in the letter.
- Put a first-class stamp (they cost 29¢) on any envelope you send. You can get stamps at the post office.
- **Neatly print** the supplier's address in the center of the envelope and your return address in the upper left-hand corner.
- If you're sending many letters at once, make sure you put the right letter in the right envelope.
- Use a ballpoint pen.

Sending a Long Self-Addressed, Stamped Envelope

If the directions say to enclose a long self-addressed, stamped envelope, here's how to do it:

- **Neatly print** your name and address in the center of a 9½-inch long envelope as if you were mailing it to yourself. Print your return address in the upper left-hand corner of the envelope as well. Put a first-class stamp on it.
- Fold up the long self-addressed, stamped envelope, and put it inside another 9½-inch long envelope (along with your letter to the supplier) and put a first-class stamp on it.
- **Neatly print** the supplier's address in the center of the envelope you are sending and your return address in the upper left-hand corner.
- Use a ballpoint pen.

Sending Money

Many of the suppliers in this book are not charging you for their items. However, the cost of postage and handling is high today, and suppliers must charge you for this. If the directions say to enclose money for postage and handling, you must do so. Here are a few rules about sending money:

- Tape the coins to your letter so they won't break out of the envelope.
- Don't stack your coins on top of each other in the envelope.
- If an item costs $1.00, send a one-dollar bill instead of coins (unless the directions say otherwise). Don't tape dollar bills.
- Send only U.S. money.
- If a grown-up is helping you, he/she may write a check (unless the directions say otherwise).
- Send all money directly to the suppliers—their addresses are listed with their offers.

Getting Your Free Stuff

Expect to wait four to eight weeks for your free stuff to arrive. Sometimes you have to wait longer. Remember, suppliers get thousands of requests each year. Please be patient! If you wait a long time and your offer still doesn't come, you may be using the wrong edition. This is the **1993** edition—the offers in this book will only be good for 1992 and 1993!

Making Sure You Get Your Request

The Free Stuff Editors have tried to make the directions for using this book as clear as possible to make sure you get what you send for. But you must follow **all** of the directions **exactly** as they're written, or the supplier will not be able to answer your request. If you're confused about the directions, ask a grown-up to help you.

Do's and Don'ts:

- **Do** use a ballpoint pen. Pencil can be difficult to read, and ink pen often smears.
- **Do** print. Cursive can be difficult to read.
- **Do** print your name, address, and zip code clearly and fully on the postcard or on the envelope **and** the letter you send. Do not abbreviate anything except state names. Abbreviations can be confusing, and sometimes envelopes and letters get separated after they reach the supplier.
- **Do** send the correct amount of U.S. money, but use as few coins as possible.
- **Do** tape the coins you send to the letter you send them with. If you don't, the money might rip the envelope and fall out.
- **Do** use a 9½-inch long self-addressed, stamped envelope if the instructions say you should.

- **Do not** ask for more than **one** of an item.
- **Do not** stack coins in the envelope.
- **Do not** ask Meadowbrook Press to send you any of the items listed in the book unless you are ordering the Meadowbrook offers from p. 24, p. 25, or p. 66. The publishers of this book do not carry items belonging to other suppliers. They do not supply refunds, either.

If you follow all the rules, you won't be disappointed!

What to Do If You Aren't Satisfied:

If you have complaints about any offer, or if you don't receive the items you sent for within eight to ten weeks, contact the Free Stuff Editors. Before you complain, please reread the directions. Are you sure you followed them properly? Are you using this **1993** edition **after** 1993? (Offers here are only good for 1992 and 1993.) The Free Stuff Editors won't be able to send you the item, but they can make sure that any suppliers who don't fulfill requests are dropped from next year's *Free Stuff for Kids*. We'd like to know which offers you like and what kind of new offers you'd like us to add to next year's edition. So don't be bashful—write us a letter. Send your complaints or suggestions to:

The Free Stuff Editors
Meadowbrook Press
18318 Minnetonka Boulevard
Deephaven, MN 55391

Free Stuff for Kids Checklist

Use this checklist each time you send out a request. It will help you follow directions exactly and prevent mistakes. Put a check mark in the box each time you complete a task—you can photocopy this page and use it again and again.

When sending postcards and letters:

❑ I used a ballpoint pen.

❑ I printed neatly and carefully.

❑ I asked for the correct item (only one).

❑ I wrote to the correct supplier.

❑ I double-checked the supplier's address.

When sending postcards only:

❑ I put my return address on the postcard.

❑ I applied a 19¢ stamp (if the postage wasn't pre-printed).

When sending letters only:

❑ I put my return address on the letter.

❑ I included a long self-addressed, stamped envelope (if the directions asked for one).

❑ I included the correct amount of money (if the directions asked for money).

❑ I put my return address on the envelope.

❑ I applied a 29¢ stamp.

When sending a long self-addressed, stamped envelope:

❑ I used a 9½-inch long envelope.

❑ I put my address on the front of the envelope.

❑ I put my return address in the upper left-hand corner of the envelope.

❑ I applied a 29¢ stamp.

When sending a one-dollar bill:

❑ I sent U.S. money.

❑ I enclosed a one-dollar bill with my letter instead of coins.

When sending coins:

❑ I sent U.S. money.

❑ I taped the coins to my letter.

❑ I did not stack the coins on top of each other.

SPORTS

Go Twins

Play ball! The 1991 World Champion Minnesota Twins have an offer you won't want to miss. Send for a Twins schedule and brochure.

Directions:	Write your request on paper, and put it in an envelope. You must enclose a long self-addressed, stamped envelope.
Write to:	Fan Mail Minnesota Twins 501 Chicago Avenue South Minneapolis, MN 55415
Ask for:	Minnesota Twins pocket schedule and novelty brochure

Sock It to 'em

White Sox fans, here's an offer for you! This sticker features the new logo of the team that finished second in the American League West in 1991.

Directions:	Write your request on paper, and put it in an envelope. You must enclose a long self-addressed, stamped envelope.
Write to:	Chicago White Sox 333 West 35th Street Chicago, IL 60616
Ask for:	Chicago White Sox logo sticker

Yankee Doodle Dandy

Batter up! One of the American League's oldest teams has an offer you'll want to swing at. Send for a New York Yankees sticker and schedule.

Directions:	Write your request on paper, and put it in an envelope. You must enclose a long self-addressed, stamped envelope.
Write to:	Community Relations Department c/o Tom Paulson New York Yankees Yankee Stadium Bronx, NY 10451
Ask for:	New York Yankees pocket schedule and logo sticker

They're G-r-r-r-eat!

This pitch is right down the pipe! The Detroit Tigers fan pack includes a colorful team sticker and schedule. You'll also get a photo of a team member or manager Sparky Anderson, the legendary skipper of the Tigers.

Directions:	Write your request on paper, and put it in an envelope. You must enclose a long self-addressed, stamped envelope.
Write to:	Fan Pack Detroit Tigers Tiger Stadium Detroit, MI 48216
Ask for:	Detroit Tigers fan pack

Home of the Braves

The winners of the 1991 National League pennant, who played in one of the greatest World Series ever, have an offer for you. This Braves fan pack includes a bumper sticker, schedule, and player photo (depending on availability).

1991 NATIONAL LEAGUE CHAMPIONS

Directions:	Write your request on paper, and put it in an envelope. You must enclose a long self-addressed, stamped envelope.
Write to:	Fan Mail Atlanta Braves P.O. Box 4064 Atlanta, GA 30302
Ask for:	Atlanta Braves bumper sticker, schedule, and player photo

Home on the Rangers

St-eee-rike! Root for the team that living legend Nolan Ryan pitches for. This Texas Rangers fan pack includes a team schedule, logo sticker, and souvenir list.

Directions:	Write your request on paper, and put it in an envelope. You must enclose a long self-addressed, stamped envelope.
Write to:	Texas Rangers Souvenirs P.O. Box 90111 Arlington, TX 76004-3111
Ask for:	Texas Rangers schedule, sticker, and souvenir list

Amazing Astros

The Houston Astros, named in honor of the astronauts and the nearby Johnson Space Center, have a great offer for baseball fans. Their fan pack features a schedule, logo sticker, and player photo.

Directions:	Write your request on paper, and put it in an envelope. You must enclose a long self-addressed, stamped envelope.
Write to:	Houston Astros Public Relations P.O. Box 288 Houston, TX 77001-0288
Ask for:	Houston Astros schedule, logo sticker, and player photo

All-New Rockies

1993 is going to be a big year for baseball with the addition of two new National League teams—one of them is the Colorado Rockies. Get ahead of the game by sending for this sticker pack that features the Rockies' great new logo and insignia. You'll get a total of eight big stickers.

Directions:	Write your request on paper, and put it in an envelope. You must enclose **$1.50.** (*We think this offer is a good value for the money.*)
Write to:	Mr. Rainbows Department K-1 P.O. Box 387 Avalon, NJ 08202
Ask for:	Colorado Rockies sticker pack

Baseball Card Mania

Which active pitcher has won the most Cy Young Awards? The answer: Roger Clemens! Baseball cards are a great way to keep track of player statistics and team information, and these cards will tell you all about your favorite players—add the cards in this pack to your collection or trade with your friends.

Directions:	Write your request on paper, and put it in an envelope. You must enclose a long self-addressed, stamped envelope and **50¢.**
Write to:	DANORS Department G 5721 Funston Street, Bay 14 Hollywood, FL 33023
Ask for:	Baseball card pack

Card Collecting Craze

Do you collect baseball cards? *Baseball Card News* is a biweekly magazine that contains the most current news, photos, and features. Send for a free sample copy.

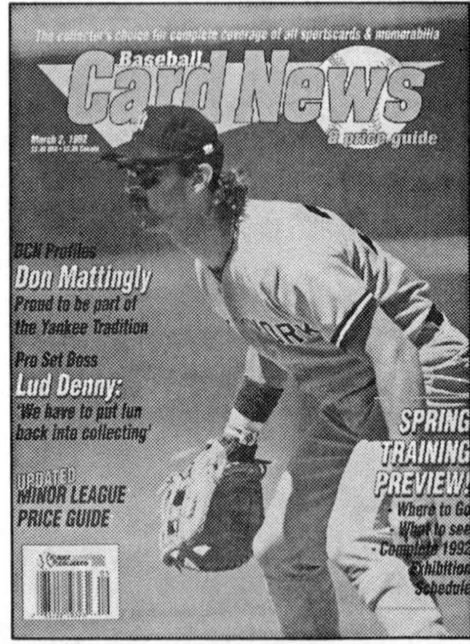

Directions:	Use a postcard.
Write to:	Baseball Card News Department BTB 700 East State Street Iola, WI 54990
Ask for:	*Baseball Card News* sample copy

Red Hot!

Celebrate the hottest game on ice. Send for this fan pack from the Detroit Red Wings, and you'll get a team photo, schedule, and merchandise catalog.

Directions:	Write your request on paper, and put it in an envelope. You must enclose a long self-addressed, stamped envelope.
Write to:	Detroit Red Wings 600 Civic Center Drive Detroit, MI 48226
Ask for:	Detroit Red Wings fan pack

Have a Whale of a Time

You'll have tons of fun with these items from the Hartford Whalers: a team poster with the message, "Winners wear safety belts," a mini calendar card featuring a photo of the team, and a schedule.

Directions:	Use a postcard.
Write to:	Hartford Whalers 242 Trumbull Street Hartford, CT 06013
Ask for:	Hartford Whalers poster, calendar card, and schedule

He Shoots! He Scores!

Take advantage of this power play offer from the New York Rangers. Their fan pack includes a player postcard, schedule, and logo sticker.

Directions:	Write your request on paper, and put it in an envelope. You must enclose a long self-addressed, stamped envelope.
Write to:	New York Rangers Marketing Department Madison Square Garden Four Pennsylvania Plaza New York, NY 10001
Ask for:	New York Rangers fan pack

A Capital Idea

"Caps" fans will love this offer from the Washington Capitals. Their fan pack includes team information sheets, a schedule, and a souvenir brochure.

Directions:	Write your request on paper, and put it in an envelope. You must enclose a long self-addressed, stamped envelope.
Write to:	Washington Capitals Capital Centre Landover, MD 20785 Attention: Fan Mail
Ask for:	Washington Capitals fan pack

En Garde!

You might be familiar with fencing–the art of sword fighting–from the stories of the Three Musketeers, Robin Hood, and Peter Pan. But did you know that fencing is a popular Olympic sport today? Send for this brochure to learn about fencing's finer points.

SPECTATOR BROCHURE

Fencing, the art of swordsmanship, has been practiced for centuries. First, it was to train for deadly combat — the Duel; then for the Olympic GOLD.

Fencing can help you acquire the reflexes of a boxer, the legs of a high-jumper, and the concentration of a tournament chess player. The sport develops your agility, strength, speed and cunning. And because it's action-packed, it's known as the fastest martial sport of them all. But the best thing about fencing is — IT'S FUN! Try it, and see why we say that nothing turns you on quite like fencing.

Directions: Write your request on paper, and put it in an envelope. You must enclose a long self-addressed, stamped envelope.

Write to: USFA
Promotional Department
1750 East Boulder Street
Colorado Springs, CO 80909-5774

Ask for: Spectator Brochure

Foiled Again!

Get this colorful United States Fencing Association decal, and show that you support young fencers who hope to enter the Olympics one day.

Directions: Write your request on paper, and put it in an envelope. You must enclose a long self-addressed, stamped envelope and **50¢.**

Write to: USFA
Promotional Department
1750 East Boulder Street
Colorado Springs, CO 80909-5774

Ask for: Fencing decal

Ski and Shoot

The biathlon is a winter Olympic sport that combines cross-country skiing and target shooting. It comes from the Scandinavian countries, but the United States also has a biathlon team. You can show your support for them by displaying this decal.

Directions:	Write your request on paper, and put it in an envelope. You must enclose **$1.00.**
Write to:	U.S. Biathlon Association Logo Sales P.O. Box 859 West Farmington, ME 04992
Ask for:	U.S. Biathlon team decal

Good as Gold

Dive right into this offer! The U.S. Swimming competition isn't just about going for the gold—it's about building a tradition that's as good as gold. Get this decal, and show your support.

Directions:	Write your request on paper, and put it in an envelope. You must enclose a long self-addressed, stamped envelope.
Write to:	United States Swimming Promotions Department 1750 East Boulder Street Colorado Springs, CO 80909-5770
Ask for:	United States Swimming logo decal

Play by the Rules

Tennis anyone? Whether you're a pro or beginner, you need to know the rules of the game. This booklet explains the rules of singles, doubles, and scoring—everything from service to set.

Directions:	Write your request on paper, and put it in an envelope. You must enclose **$1.00.**
Write to:	USTA Publications 707 Alexander Road Princeton, NJ 08540
Ask for:	Summarized Rules of Tennis booklet

Get on the Ball

Be a good sport on the tennis court! If you're serious about tennis, get familiar with the Tennis Code of Conduct. Learn how to keep your cool on the court, and opponents and spectators will appreciate your good sportsmanship.

Directions:	Write your request on paper, and put it in an envelope. You must enclose **25¢.**
Write to:	USTA Publications 707 Alexander Road Princeton, NJ 08540
Ask for:	Tennis Code of Conduct card

Get Fit!

Arnold Schwarzenegger and the President want you to get physically fit. You can take the Presidential Sports Award challenge by participating in sports ranging from football to ice skating. Find out about all the cool awards you can receive if you succeed. (For ages 10 and up.)

Directions:	Write your request on paper, and put it in an envelope. You must enclose a long self-addressed, stamped envelope.
Write to:	Presidential Sports Award P.O. Box 68207 Indianapolis, IN 46268
Ask for:	Presidential Sports Award pamphlet

Don't Rock the Cradle

Go for the goal with this exciting magazine from the Lacrosse Foundation. *Lacrosse* will explain everything from "cradling" to who's who in the sport.

Directions:	Write your request on paper, and put it in an envelope. You must enclose **$1.00.**
Write to:	The Lacrosse Foundation 113 West University Parkway Baltimore, MD 21210
Ask for:	*Lacrosse* magazine sample

Water Skiing Is Wild!

Giving the thumbs-down sign when you're water skiing doesn't mean you're not having a good time—it signals the boat driver to slow down. Learn more about proper signaling and safety from this illustrated booklet.

Directions:	Write your request on paper, and put it in an envelope. You must enclose a long self-addressed, stamped envelope.
Write to:	American Water Ski Association 799 Overlook Drive Winter Haven, FL 33884
Ask for:	Guide to Safe Water Skiing booklet

Right up Your Alley

Do you know how to throw a strike or convert a spare? This foldout shows you how to do that and more! You can also send for *Framework* magazine, which contains fun information about young people involved in the sport.

Directions:	Write your request on paper, and put it in an envelope. You must enclose a long self-addressed, stamped envelope for the foldout. *Framework* is free—use a postcard.
Write to:	Young American Bowling Alliance 5301 South 76th Street Greendale, WI 53129
Ask for:	· Bif's Fun-Damentals of Bowling foldout · YABA *Framework* magazine

FREE

Derby Days

On your mark, get set, go! Get the latest Official All-American Soap Box Derby Activities Book, and learn about entering contests and winning soap box derbies.

Directions:	Use a postcard.
Write to:	All-American Soap Box Derby P. O. Box 7233 Derby Downs Akron, OH 44306
Ask for:	The Official All-American Soap Box Derby Activities Book

Lost and Found

Orienteering is finding your way, using only a map and compass, along an unknown stretch of ground. It's a challenging way to learn about the land, nature, and yourself. This booklet and sample topographic map will help you get started.

Directions:	Write your request on paper, and put it in an envelope. You must enclose a long self-addressed, stamped envelope.
Write to:	Silva Orienteering Services, USA Department FS P. O. Box 1604 Binghamton, NY 13902
Ask for:	Orienteering map and booklet

READING

Betcha Laugh

Who says poetry can't be fun? *Kids Pick the Funniest Poems* is an illustrated book full of hilarious poems chosen by kids your age—you'll find your favorite poets in it! Send for this pamphlet featuring eight of the poems in the book, and get ready to laugh out loud.

Directions:	Write your request on paper, and put it in an envelope. You must enclose a long self-addressed, stamped envelope and **25¢.**
Write to:	Meadowbrook Press Department FP 18318 Minnetonka Boulevard Deephaven, MN 55391
Ask for:	Funny Poetry pamphlet

Pick a Poster

Now you can really make your bedroom look beautiful. You'll get a poster featuring a scene from a great new children's book drawn by a famous children's book illustrator.

Directions:	Write your request on paper, and put it in an envelope. You must enclose **two 29¢** stamps.
Write to:	The Putnam & Grosset Group Department LCF 200 Madison Avenue New York, NY 10016
Ask for:	Children's book poster

Super Suspense

Can you solve the mystery? Suspense lovers will go nuts for these short mysteries that you solve yourself. Super Sleuths Amy and Hawkeye get involved in nine different mysteries in this exciting 100-page book.

Directions:	Write your request on paper, and put it in an envelope. You must enclose **$1.00.**
Write to:	Meadowbrook Press Department CYSM 18318 Minnetonka Boulevard Deephaven, MN 55391
Ask for:	*Loon Lake Monster* mystery book

"Soup-er" Writing

If you love writing or drawing pictures, *Stone Soup* is the magazine for you. Every issue contains stories, poems, book reviews, and artwork by kids ages 6 to 13 from all over the world. It's a great way to find out about other kids and to get some creative inspiration.

Directions:	Write your request on paper (*include your name and address*), and put it in an envelope. You must enclose **$1.00.**
Write to:	Stone Soup P.O. Box 83 Santa Cruz, CA 95063
Ask for:	Sample copy of *Stone Soup* magazine

BOOKMARKS

Don't Lose Your Place!

You'll never lose your place if you mark your page with a bookmark. You'll get two bookmarks with colorful scenes from popular new Putnam & Grosset children's books.

Directions:	Write your request on paper, and put it in an envelope. You must enclose a long self-addressed, stamped envelope.
Write to:	The Putnam & Grosset Group Department LCF 200 Madison Avenue New York, NY 10016
Ask for:	Two free bookmarks

Read All about It!

Want some information about Simon & Schuster's great new children's books? You'll get an illustrated postcard or two colorful bookmarks—it's a surprise!

Directions:	Write your request on paper, and put it in an envelope. You must enclose a long self-addressed, stamped envelope.
Write to:	Simon & Schuster Children's Books 15 Columbus Circle New York, NY 10023 Attention: Marketing Department
Ask for:	Free book stuff

Young Readers

Explore these exciting magazines by yourself or with a grown-up.

- *Turtle* (ages 2 to 5) is a unique magazine filled with read-to-me stories, hidden pictures, dot-to-dots, coloring pages, and more.
- *Humpty Dumpty's* (ages 4 to 6) entertains and teaches with fun stories, poems, puzzles, and crafts.
- *Children's Playmate* (ages 6 to 8) offers colorfully illustrated stories for beginning readers, intriguing puzzles, games, recipes, cartoons, and activities.

Directions:	Write your request on paper, and put it in an envelope. You must enclose **$1.00** for **each** magazine you request.
Write to:	J.A. Aydt, Samples "S" Children's Better Health Institute P.O. Box 567 Indianapolis, IN 46206
Ask for:	· *Turtle* magazine · *Humpty Dumpty's* magazine · *Children's Playmate* magazine

Older Readers

These three magazines for older readers invite you to learn, laugh, and create.

- *Jack and Jill* (ages 7 to 10) entertains with illustrated fiction, jokes, activities—plus works by kids.
- *Child Life* (ages 9 to 11) offers Diane's Dinosaur comics, Odd Job career profiles, activities, and great stories.
- *Children's Digest* (preteen) features contemporary fiction, articles on important issues, challenging puzzles, book reviews, and cartoons.

Directions:	Write your request on paper, and put it in an envelope. You must enclose **$1.00** for **each** magazine you request.
Write to:	J.A. Aydt, Samples "S" Children's Better Health Institute P.O. Box 567 Indianapolis, IN 46206
Ask for:	• *Jack and Jill* magazine • *Child Life* magazine • *Children's Digest* magazine

SCHOOL SUPPLIES

Batter Up!

What kind of baseball bat can you use in class? One that's really a pen! This mini baseball bat pen is autographed by superstar Ryne Sandberg of the Chicago Cubs.

Directions:	Write your request on paper, and put it in an envelope. You must enclose **$1.00.**
Write to:	H & B Promotions Department 90 SRC P. O. Box 10 Jeffersonville, IN 47130
Ask for:	Louisville Slugger bat pen

Wrist Writer

You'll always have handy handwriting with this flexible pen bracelet.

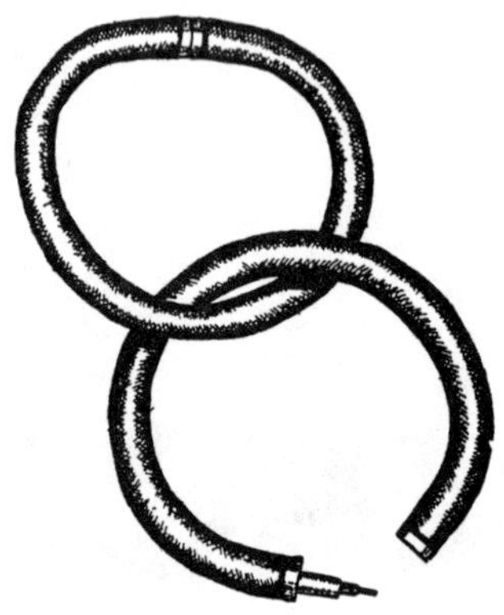

Directions:	Write your request on paper, and put it in an envelope. You must enclose a long self-addressed, stamped envelope and **$1.00.**
Write to:	Neetstuf Department N-3 P.O. Box 207 Glenside, PA 19038
Ask for:	Pen bracelet

M-M-Good Memos

Send a "sweet" note to someone special. These two memo pads feature delicious treats on every page.

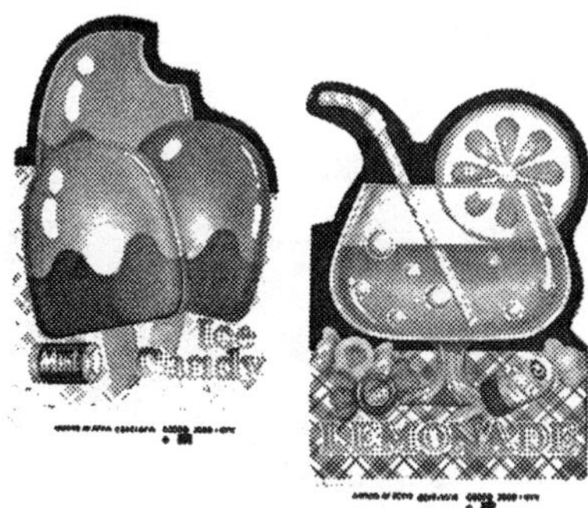

Directions:	Write your request on paper, and put it in an envelope. You must enclose a long self-addressed, stamped envelope and **$1.00.**
Write to:	Mr. Rainbows Department K-2 P.O. Box 387 Avalon, NJ 08202
Ask for:	Two "yummy" memo pads

Dig These Dinosaurs

These mini memo pads are great for taking notes in class or writing notes to your friends. Each cover features a different cartoon dinosaur. You'll get three.

Directions:	Write your request on paper, and put it in an envelope. You must enclose **$1.00.**
Write to:	Eleanor Curran Department MM 530 Leonard Street Brooklyn, NY 11222
Ask for:	Three dinosaur mini memo pads

Over the Rainbow

Your school box isn't complete without a few erasers. These multi-colored erasers are shaped like "love-ly" little hearts. You'll get three.

Directions:	Write your request on paper, and put it in an envelope. You must enclose a long self-addressed, stamped envelope and **$1.00.**
Write to:	Mr. Rainbows Department K-6 P.O. Box 387 Avalon, NJ 08202
Ask for:	Three rainbow heart erasers

Enormous Erasers

These giant erasers will last a long, long time. You'll get a fabulous fish and a lazy-looking alligator.

Directions:	Write your request on paper, and put it in an envelope. You must enclose a long self-addressed, stamped envelope and **$1.00.**
Write to:	DANORS Department G 5721 Funston Street, Bay 14 Hollywood, FL 33023
Ask for:	Giant fish and alligator erasers

Under Cover

Your favorite dog detective, McGruff the Crime Dog, wants to tell you and your friends to say "no" to drugs. Cover your books with this message, and take a bite out of crime. Other book cover choices include "dinosaurs" or a "rainbow scene."

Directions:	Write your request on paper, and put it in an envelope. You must enclose **$1.00** for **each** cover you request.
Write to:	Mr. Rainbows Department K-7 P.O. Box 387 Avalon, NJ 08202
Ask for:	· McGruff book cover · Dinosaurs book cover · Rainbow Scene book cover

Math in a Flash

How can a ruler help you with math? When it has a multiplication table printed on it! Tilt this mini ruler one way and you'll see the problems. Tilt it the other way and you'll see the answers.

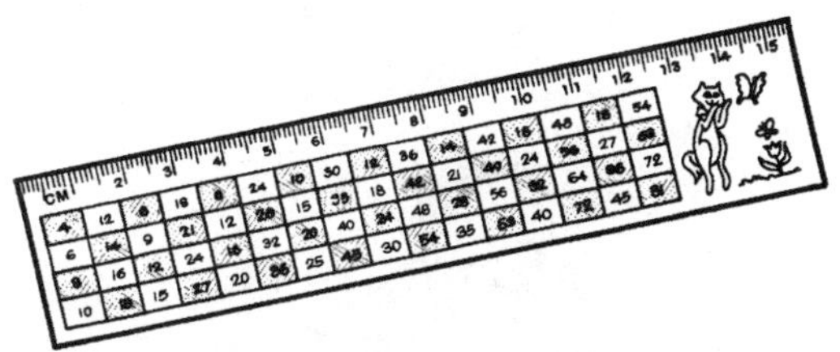

Directions:	Write your request on paper, and put it in an envelope. You must enclose a long self-addressed, stamped envelope and **$1.00.**
Write to:	IPM Department M-4 P.O. Box 1181 Hammond, IN 46325
Ask for:	Just-a-Twist ruler

Great Skate

Keep your change in a roller skate. This colorful vinyl purse looks like a little roller skate, but it has room for your lunch money or other stuff you need to take with you.

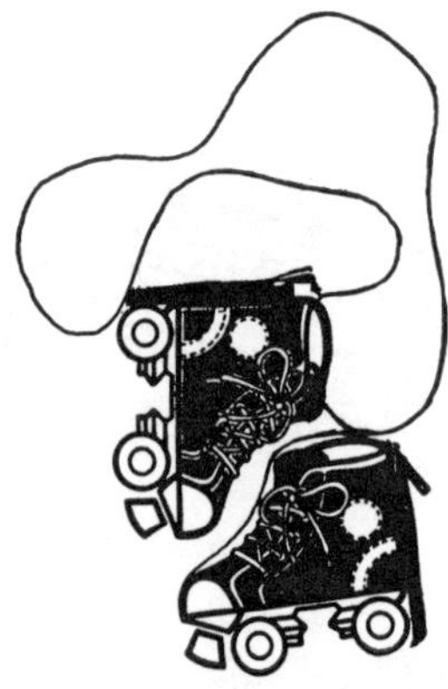

Directions:	Write your request on paper, and put it in an envelope. You must enclose **$1.00.**
Write to:	Eleanor Curran Department FS 530 Leonard Street Brooklyn, NY 11222
Ask for:	Roller skate coin purse

Pouch Power

This flourescent mini wrist pouch with a Velcro strap is perfect for kids on the go. Carry any small personal items with you during lunch, recess, or after-school sports.

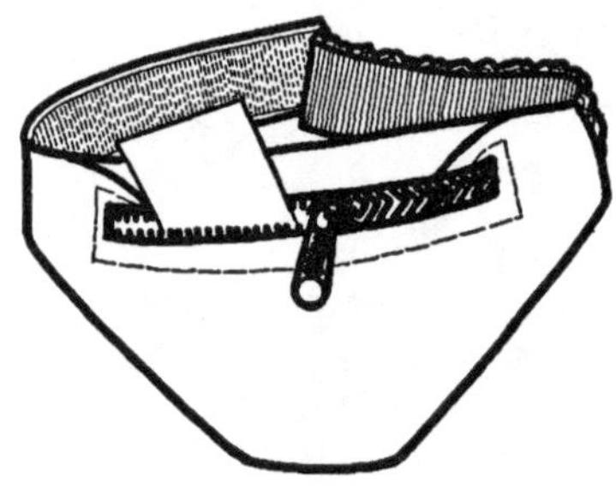

Directions:	Write your request on paper, and put it in an envelope. You must enclose a long self-addressed, stamped envelope and **$1.00.**
Write to:	The Complete Traveler 490 Route 46 East Fairfield, NJ 07006
Ask for:	Mini wrist pouch

Picture This

Add a little magnetism to your life! Have a favorite photo mounted on a button magnet, and stick it on your locker or a friend's.

Directions:	Write your request on paper (*include a photo*), and put it in an envelope. You must enclose a long self-addressed, stamped envelope and **$1.00.**
Write to:	Professor Bob 135 Echo Drive Chambersburg, PA 17201
Ask for:	Photo magnet button

U.S.A. Magnets

Now you can have a magnet with your home state stamp on it. Collect all fifty plus the District of Columbia for a full set.

Directions:	Write your request on paper, and put it in an envelope. You must enclose **75¢** for **each** magnet you request.
Write to:	Hicks Specialties 1308 68th Lane North Brooklyn Center, MN 55430
Ask for:	State stamp magnet (*specify the state you want*)

Big Bat Key-Keeper

Keep your keys on something cool—a Major League key chain. This mini Louisville Slugger bat is autographed by Wade Boggs, the great Boston Red Sox All-Star.

Directions:	Write your request on paper, and put it in an envelope. You must enclose **$1.00.**
Write to:	H & B Promotions Department 90 SRC P. O. Box 10 Jeffersonville, IN 47130
Ask for:	Louisville Slugger bat key chain

Framing Fun

Here are two key chains that double as picture frames when you insert your favorite photos. These 2-by-2 inch heart-shaped frames are colorful and durable.

Directions:	Write your request on paper, and put it in an envelope. You must enclose a long self-addressed, stamped envelope and **$1.00.** *(Please **do not** send photographs.)*
Write to:	Mr. Rainbows Department P-1 P.O. Box 387 Avalon, NJ 08202
Ask for:	Two picture frame key chains

THE ENVIRONMENT

Think Green

It's your earth, too, so help make it last! Put this environmental awareness sticker on your notebooks, folders, and memo pads to remind you not to waste paper—this will save trees and help keep the planet green. You'll get a set of twenty stickers.

IT'S YOUR
EARTH TOO!
Please help
keep it
GREEN!

Directions:	Write your request on paper, and put it in an envelope. You must enclose a long self-addressed, stamped envelope and **$1.00.**
Write to:	Fax Marketing Department FS 460 Carrollton Drive Frederick, MD 21701-6357
Ask for:	Environment stickers

Save the Earth

Kids like you are doing a lot to save Mother Earth. Join the environmental club that sixth-grader Clinton Hill started, and learn how to make the planet a healthier, happier place for future generations. Send for a Kids for Saving Earth® sticker and club information.

Kids for SAVing Earth™
the Pollution solution

Directions:	Write your request on paper, and put it in an envelope. You must enclose **$1.00.**
Write to:	Kids for Saving Earth Department F P.O. Box 47247 Plymouth, MN 55447
Ask for:	KSE sticker and club information

Stick Up for the Planet!

These stickers are fun and practical. They include trees, rain, and the earth in bright colors to help you remember to save the environment.

Directions:	Write your request on paper, and put it in an envelope. You must enclose a long self-addressed, stamped envelope and **$1.00.**
Write to:	Mr. Rainbows Department K-9 P.O. Box 387 Avalon, NJ 08202
Ask for:	Mylar environment stickers

Give the Earth a Hug!

Show everyone that you care about the environment. These fuzzy stickers feature teddy bears hugging the earth.

Directions:	Write your request on paper, and put it in an envelope. You must enclose a long self-addressed, stamped envelope and **$1.00.**
Write to:	Mr. Rainbows Department P-2 P.O. Box 387 Avalon, NJ 08202
Ask for:	Fuzzy earth stickers

Take Out the Garbage

Litter is a widespread problem, but you can take the initiative to make the world a cleaner place. This fact sheet provides information on how to get rid of the litter that pollutes our earth.

Directions:	Write your request on paper, and put it in an envelope. You must enclose a long self-addressed, stamped envelope.
Write to:	Keep America Beautiful Mill River Plaza 9 West Broad Street Stamford, CT 06902
Ask for:	Litter Tips fact sheet

Take Pride in America

Help forge a trail to a cleaner environment. This coloring book, featuring comic strip character Mark Trail, will teach you about taking good care of our wildlife and public lands.

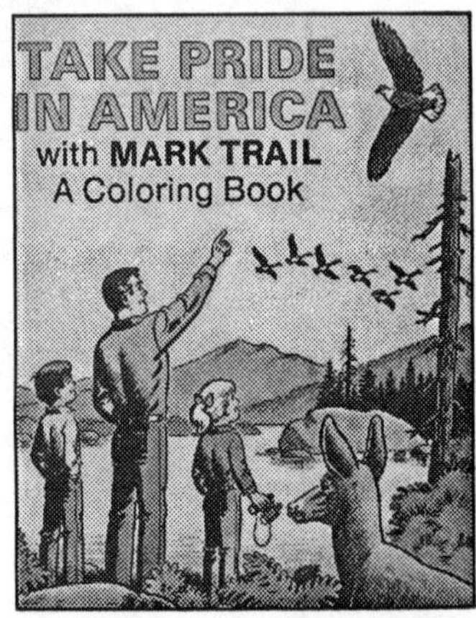

Directions:	Write your request on paper, and put it in an envelope. You must enclose **50¢.**
Write to:	Consumer Information Center Department 416Y Pueblo, CO 81009
Ask for:	Take Pride in America coloring book

Pollution Solutions

Let's clean up the earth! This mini booklet is filled with earth-saving ideas and activities just for kids. You'll learn how to stop pollution and help the environment through fun projects you can do at home.

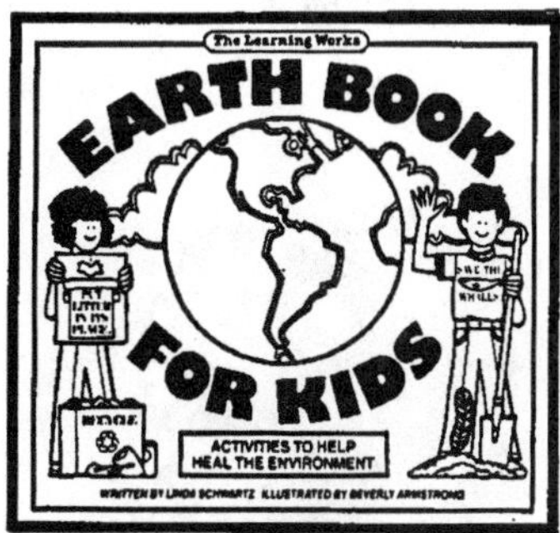

Directions:	Write your request on paper, and put it in an envelope. You must enclose a long self-addressed, stamped envelope and **50¢.**
Write to:	The Learning Works Department FSFK P.O. Box 6187 Santa Barbara, CA 93160
Ask for:	Earth Book for Kids mini booklet

Give a Hoot . . .

Don't pollute! Show the world that you're not a litterbug. Wear this "Keep America Beautiful" patch to remind you and your friends to protect the environment from all forms of pollution.

Directions:	Write your request on paper, and put it in an envelope. You must enclose a long self-addressed, stamped envelope and **$1.25.** (*We think this offer is a good value for the money.*)
Write to:	Keep America Beautiful Mill River Plaza 9 West Broad Street Stamford, CT 06902
Ask for:	Keep America Beautiful patch

"KIND" of Special

What do endangered animals, recycling, conservation, rock stars, sports figures, and kindness have in common? You'll find them all in *KIND News!* This classroom newspaper shows you how to be kind to animals, people, and the earth.

Directions:	Write your request on paper, and put it in an envelope. You must enclose **75¢** for **each** newspaper you request.
Write to:	KIND News Department FS 67 Salem Road East Haddam, CT 06423-1736
Ask for:	· *KIND News Jr.* (grades 2–4) · *KIND News Sr.* (grades 5–6)

Take Action!

Ever wonder what you can do to help save the environment? *The HSUS Student Action Guide* has lots of suggestions for forming your own earth and animal protection club. This fun newspaper from the Humane Society of the United States explains how to form a club, hold meetings, target issues, and plan activities.

Directions:	Use a postcard.
Write to:	HSUS Youth Education Division Department FS 67 Salem Road East Haddam, CT 06423-1736
Ask for:	*HSUS Student Action Guide*

Environmental Trading Cards

The earth's good fortune depends on you! These trading cards contain tips for preserving the environment and protecting wildlife, plus a special fortune just for you. Collect a bunch, and trade them with your friends.

Directions:	Write your request on paper, and put it in an envelope. You must enclose a long self-addressed, stamped envelope and **25¢** for **each** card you request.
Write to:	Good Medicine 1420 NW Gilman Boulevard, Suite 2602 Issaquah, WA 98027
Ask for:	EarthScope™ card

Sun Power

Learn all about solar power and other forms of safe and clean energy. The Conservation and Renewable Energy Inquiry Referral Service (CAREIRS) has four fact sheets to send you about renewable energy. Specify which fact sheets you want.

Directions:	Use a postcard.
Write to:	CAREIRS P.O. Box 8900 Silver Spring, MD 20907
Ask for:	· Solar Energy and You—FS 118 · Learning about Energy Conservation—FS 218 · Types of Solar Collectors—FS 112 · Passive Solar Heating—FS 121

Sunny Side Up

Now you can cook a hot dog without using a stove or microwave! These instructions on how to build a solar-powered hot dog cooker will please anyone interested in solar energy activities.

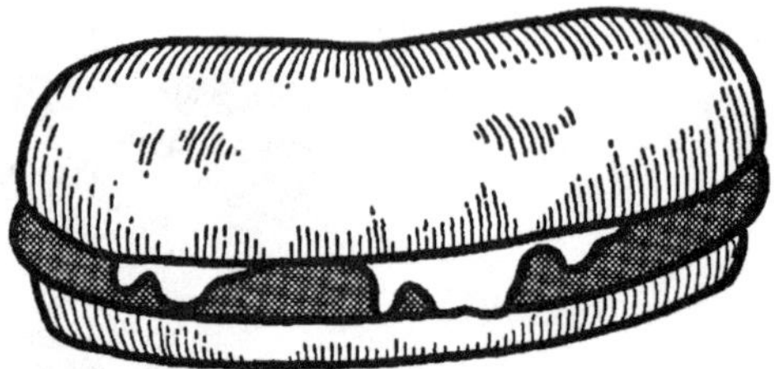

Directions:	Write your request on paper, and put it in an envelope. You must enclose a long self-addressed, stamped envelope and **25¢.**
Write to:	Energy and Marine Center P.O. Box 190 9130 Old Post Road Port Richey, FL 34673
Ask for:	Solar hot dog cooker directions

Ready to Recycle

You can help save the planet. Learn about recycling aluminum, glass, plastic, paper, and more in this coloring and activity book that's printed on recycled paper.

Directions:	Write your request on paper, and put it in an envelope. You must enclose **$1.00.**
Write to:	Special Products Department FS P.O. Box 6605 Delray Beach, FL 33484
Ask for:	Keep Your World Beautiful coloring and activity book

Reduce, Reuse, Recycle

Recycling is a great way to clean up the environment and save energy. You can learn all about recycling by reading this pamphlet from the Ohio Department of Natural Resources.

Directions:	Write your request on paper, and put it in an envelope. You must enclose a long self-addressed, stamped envelope.
Write to:	Ohio Department of Natural Resources Publications Center 4383 Fountain Square Drive Columbus, OH 43224
Ask for:	Reduce, Reuse, Recycle pamphlet

Get Earth Wise

It's important to conserve water so that crops, trees, animals, people, and other life forms can live and grow. "Ernie the Earthwise Owl" wants you to learn about water conservation in this coloring and activity book that features tips for saving water.

Directions:	Write your request on paper, and put it in an envelope. You must enclose **$1.00.**
Write to:	Special Products Department FS P.O. Box 6605 Delray Beach, FL 33484
Ask for:	Helping Our Community Save Water coloring book

Adopt a Stream

Our streams are in trouble, but you can help. Adopt a stream in your neighborhood, and become a "streamkeeper." These sheets explain how to preserve streams so they stay safe for fish, wildlife, and recreational activities. You'll also get a button with a colorful fish on it.

Directions:	Write your request on paper, and put it in an envelope. You must enclose a long self-addressed, stamped envelope and **$1.00.**
Write to:	Adopt-A-Stream Foundation P.O. Box 5558 Everett, WA 98206
Ask for:	Adopt-A-Stream information sheets and fish button

Let There Be Trees

Trees help convert carbon dioxide in the air into the oxygen that we need to breathe. They also provide valuable shade, shelter, and food for many living things. "Trees for Life" wants to promote awareness of this valuable resource—send for their bumper sticker, button, or free coloring sheet.

Directions:	Write your request on paper, and put it in an envelope. You must enclose a long self-addressed, stamped envelope for the coloring sheet, **$1.00** for the button, and/or **$1.00** for the bumper sticker.
Write to:	Trees for Life "Kids" Offer 1103 Jefferson Wichita, KS 67203-3559
Ask for:	· Coloring sheet · Button · Bumper sticker

Plant a Tree

This tree growing kit contains everything you need to grow a tree—just add water and sunlight!

Directions:	Write your request on paper, and put it in an envelope. You must enclose **$2.00 in check or money order—do not send cash.** (*We think this offer is a good value for the money.*)
Write to:	Free Stuff Growing Kit P.O. Box 5683 Stacy, MN 55079
Ask for:	Tree Growing Kit

CONSERVATION

This Land Is Your Land

Learn all about conservation with these water and soil pamphlets:

- **Flood Plain Management**–This illustrated pamphlet discusses how to prevent flooding and the resulting damage.
- **Grass Makes Its Own Food**–This illustrated pamphlet explains how this "taken for granted" plant grows. It folds out into a poster for your room.
- **Going Wild with Soil and Water Conservation**–This colorful 23-page booklet describes many soil and water conservation practices that can benefit wildlife.
- **Mulches for Your Garden**–This illustrated pamphlet describes how using mulch can help the soil and your garden thrive.

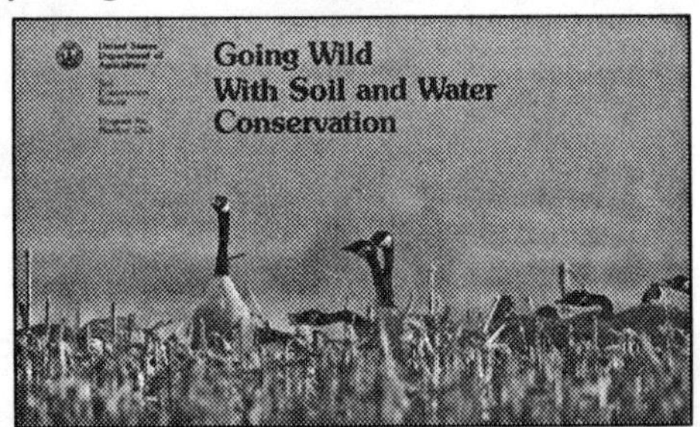

Directions:	Write your request on paper, and put it in an envelope. You must enclose a long self-addressed, stamped envelope for **each** pamphlet you request.
Write to:	U.S. Department of Agriculture Soil Conservation Service, Room 0054-S P.O. Box 2890 Washington, DC 20013
Ask for:	Name of the pamphlet you want

ANIMAL KINGDOM

Be a Bird-Watcher

Bird-watching is a fun hobby for people of all ages. And you don't have to go any further than your own backyard! This pamphlet tells you how to build or buy your own birdhouse.

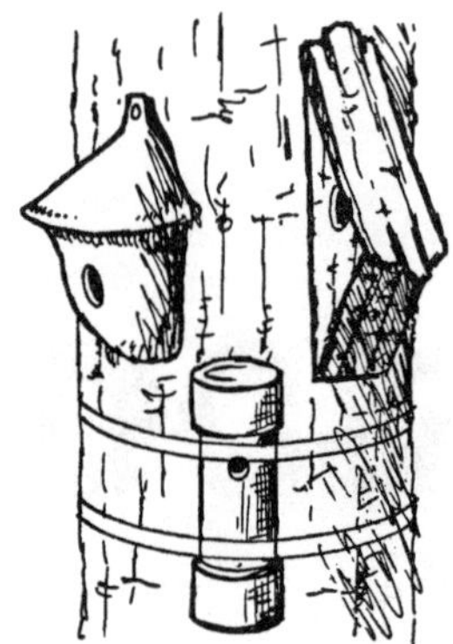

Directions:	Use a postcard.
Write to:	Consumer Information Center Department 584Y Pueblo, CO 81009
Ask for:	Homes for Birds pamphlet

For the Birds

You can have birds in your backyard all year round. All you need to know is what type of feeder and birdseed to buy. This pamphlet will get you started.

Directions:	Use a postcard.
Write to:	Consumer Information Center Department 582Y Pueblo, CO 81009
Ask for:	Backyard Bird Feeding pamphlet

Bird Lovers

If you love your pet bird, you should read this educational booklet called "Vital Information about Pet Birds." It tells you about the kind of environment, nutrition, and emergency care different pet birds need.

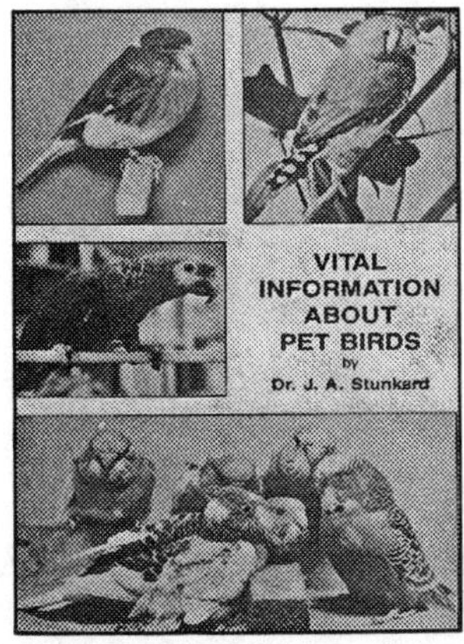

Directions:	Write your request on paper, and put it in an envelope. You must enclose **$1.00.**
Write to:	American Cage-Bird Magazine Department M One Glamore Court Smithtown, NY 11787
Ask for:	Vital Information about Pet Birds booklet

Pampered Pets

A pet is a member of your family, so it's important to give it proper care. This pamphlet tells you what a veterinary exam is all about. You'll also get a sticker with a cat, dog, and bird on it to show that you're a kid who cares about pets.

Directions:	Write your request on paper, and put it in an envelope. You must enclose a long self-addressed, stamped envelope.
Write to:	American Animal Hospital Association P.O. Box 150899 Denver, CO 80215-0899 Attention: MSC
Ask for:	Health Exams pamphlet and Caring Kids sticker

Caring for Cats

Are you a cat lover? Then you'll love this "purr-fectly" wonderful bumper sticker from the Cat Fanciers' Association. It features helpful information on cat care.

The Cat Fanciers'

Association, Inc.

Help Your Cat Live Longer
- ***Keep Your Cat Indoors***
- ***Neuter & Spay Your Pet***

It's the Humane Way!

Directions:	Write your request on paper, and put it in an envelope. You must enclose a long self-addressed, stamped envelope and **50¢.**
Write to:	Bumper Sticker The Cat Fanciers' Association 918 Millard Court West Daytona Beach, FL 32117-4217
Ask for:	Bumper sticker

Puppy Love

It's important to take good care of your new puppy or dog so he stays healthy and happy. Learn about proper canine care in these three pamphlets and fun coloring book.

Directions:	Write your request on paper, and put it in an envelope. You must enclose a long self-addressed, stamped envelope for **each** pamphlet you request. The coloring book is free—use a postcard.
Write to:	ALPO Pet Center P.O. Box 25200 Lehigh Valley, PA 18002-5200
Ask for:	· Your Courteous Canine pamphlet · Puppy Proof Your Home pamphlet · Puppies, Parents, and Kids pamphlet · You and Your Puppy coloring book

Horsing Around

In the old days, families drove to church or across country in carriages drawn by harness horses. Today these Standardbreds are used for the sport of harness racing. If you're into horses, send for this informative magazine and fun coloring book.

Directions:	Use a postcard.
Write to:	U.S. Trotting Association 750 Michigan Avenue Columbus, OH 43215-1191 Attention: Coloring Book Department
Ask for:	The Story of Harness Racing coloring book and *Hoof Beats* magazine

Horse Sense

The high-stepping Saddlebreds, known for their grace and personality, gained fame during the Civil War when they served as mounts for famous generals like Lee and Grant. This offer includes a coloring poster, a logo sticker, and informative brochures.

Directions:	Write your request on paper, and put it in an envelope. You must enclose **$1.00.**
Write to:	ASHA Department S 4093 Iron Works Pike Lexington, KY 40511
Ask for:	Coloring poster, brochures, and sticker

A Horse, of Course

If you're crazy about horses, you'll love this new offer from the American Quarter Horse Association: a colorful poster to hang in your bedroom and a matching postcard to send to a friend with an interest in horses. You'll also get a booklet and membership application for the American Junior Quarter Horse Association.

Directions:	Write your request on paper, and put it in an envelope. You must enclose **$1.00.**
Write to:	AQHA Department FS P.O. Box 200 Amarillo, TX 79168
Ask for:	American Quarter Horse poster, postcard, and booklet

For Horse Lovers

The Palomino, with its rich gold coat and snowy white tail, has been highly prized by royalty and continues to have international appeal. Send for this brochure that contains information about Palomino enthusiasts, showing, and registration.

Directions:	Write your request on paper, and put it in an envelope. You must enclose a long self-addressed, stamped envelope and **50¢.**
Write to:	Palomino Horse Breeders of America Department FS 15253 East Skelly Drive Tulsa, OK 74116-2620
Ask for:	Invest in Gold brochure

Awesome Arabians

The versatile Arabian horse can do it all—halter, western, hunter, English, trail, dressage, and jumping! The International Arabian Horse Association has lots of information about this beautiful breed of horse. You can also get a large wall chart featuring all the parts of the horse.

Directions:	Write your request on paper, and put it in an envelope. You must enclose **$1.00** if you request the wall chart.
Write to:	IAHA Department Y P.O. Box 33696 Denver, CO 80233-0696
Ask for:	• General Information packet • Parts of the Horse wall chart

Easy Riders

The Tennessee Walking Horse is the only breed of horse to bear a state name. It's famous for its free and easy gait, too. Learn all about the Tennessee Walker's history, gait, and showing ability in these pamphlets. You'll also get a big, colorful postcard featuring three famous Walkers.

Directions:	Write your request on paper, and put it in an envelope. You must enclose a long self-addressed, stamped envelope.
Write to:	Tennessee Walking Horse P.O. Box 286 Lewisburg, TN 37091
Ask for:	Postcard and two pamphlets

FREE

Wildlife Wisdom

Did you know that animals rarely abandon their babies? Learn all sorts of facts about orphaned animals, fishing, and building bluebird houses in these three pamphlets by the Ohio Department of Natural Resources.

Directions:	Write your request on paper, and put it in an envelope. You must enclose a long self-addressed, stamped envelope for **each** pamphlet you request.
Write to:	Ohio Department of Natural Resources Publications Center 4383 Fountain Square Drive Columbus, OH 43224
Ask for:	· Hit the Trail for Bluebirds pamphlet · Animal Orphans? No! pamphlet · Fishing FUNdamentals pamphlet

Living with Animals

This large coloring poster is filled with people and animals living peacefully together in homes, at the zoo, on the farm, and in the woods. Color it, and display it in your room!

Directions:	Write your request on paper, and put it in an envelope. You must enclose **75¢.**
Write to:	MSPCA—Humane Education Department LACP 350 South Huntington Avenue Boston, MA 02130
Ask for:	Living with Animals poster

STICKERS

Glow in the Dark

By day they look like ordinary stickers; by night they have a mysterious glow! These ghoulish and goofy glow-in-the-dark stickers will add a spooky shine to your collection. You'll get one sheet with critters and one with moons.

Directions:	Write your request on paper, and put it in an envelope. You must enclose a long self-addressed, stamped envelope and **$1.00.**
Write to:	Mr. Rainbows Department P-C P.O. Box 387 Avalon, NJ 08202
Ask for:	Glow-in-the-dark critters and moons

Fuzzy Animals

These colorful animal stickers are soft and fuzzy—just like real animals! Choose from pets like cats, dogs, or guinea pigs; farm animals like cows, goats, or pigs; or wild animals like raccoons, seals, or koala bears. Pick any two different animal sheets.

Directions:	Write your request on paper, and put it in an envelope. You must enclose a long self-addressed, stamped envelope and **$1.00.**
Write to:	Mr. Rainbows Department P-4 P.O. Box 387 Avalon, NJ 08202
Ask for:	Fuzzy animal stickers (*pick any two animals*)

Fast Food

Feeling hungry? This sticker sheet features rainbow-colored hot dogs, burgers, pizza, and shakes.

Directions:	Write your request on paper, and put it in an envelope. You must enclose a long self-addressed, stamped envelope and **$1.00.**
Write to:	Mr. Rainbows Department K-5 P.O. Box 387 Avalon, NJ 08202
Ask for:	Rainbow sticker sheet

Enjoy Coca-Cola

"Trink Coca-Cola" is German for "Drink Coca-Cola." This sticker postcard features the Coke trademark in six different foreign languages, including German, Russian, and Chinese.

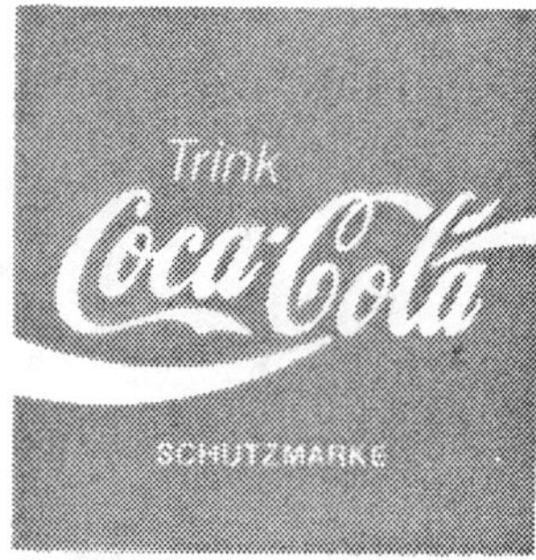

Germany

Directions:	Use a postcard.
Write to:	Coca-Cola U.S.A. Consumer Information Center Department FS P.O. Drawer 1734 Atlanta, GA 30301
Ask for:	Coca-Cola sticker postcard (*limit* **one** *per request*)

Plenty of Prisms

These colorful stickers bend the light so that they shine like a prism. Each sheet contains a variety of stickers such as unicorns, rainbows, balloons, pandas, and more!

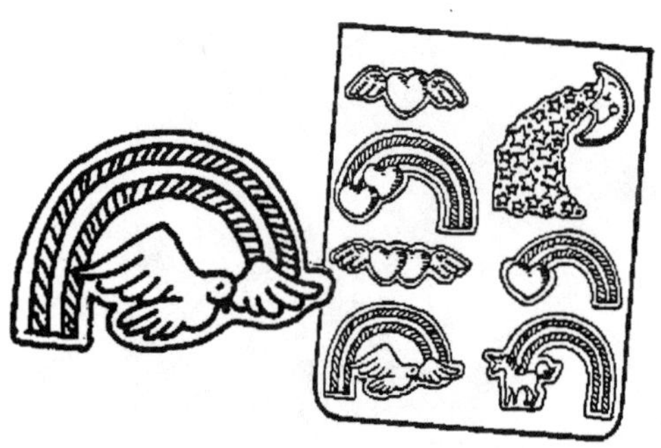

Directions:	Write your request on paper, and put it in an envelope. You must enclose **$1.00.**
Write to:	Expressions Department FSK 1668 Valtec Lane, Suite F Boulder, CO 80301
Ask for:	Prism sticker sheet

Happenin' Holograms

When the light hits these hologram stickers, watch the 3-D rainbow effect! You'll get four large stickers featuring wild animals.

Directions:	Write your request on paper, and put it in an envelope. You must enclose **$1.00.**
Write to:	Expressions Department HS 1668 Valtec Lane, Suite F Boulder, CO 80301
Ask for:	Four hologram stickers

Cowabunga!

Are you a big fan of Leonardo, Michaelangelo, Raphael, and Donatello; Mario and Luigi; Barbie and Ken; or Fred and Barney? These big, colorful sticker sheets feature all your favorite characters.

Directions:	Write your request on paper, and put it in an envelope. You must enclose a long self-addressed, stamped envelope and **$1.00** for **each** sheet you request.
Write to:	Mr. Rainbows Department 207 P.O. Box 387 Avalon, NJ 08202
Ask for:	· Teenage Mutant Ninja Turtles sticker sheet · Super Mario Brothers sticker sheet · Barbie and Ken sticker sheet · Flintstones sticker sheet

Holy Decals, Batman!

Sok! Biff! Kapow! America's caped crusader is here! This sticker sheet features the amazing Batman in five different crime-fighting poses, the famous "Bat Signal," and a few scary bats, too.

Directions:	Write your request on paper, and put it in an envelope. You must enclose a long self-addressed, stamped envelope and **$1.00.**
Write to:	Mr. Rainbows Department P-5 P.O. Box 387 Avalon, NJ 08202
Ask for:	Batman sticker sheet

Caped Crusader

Spring into action with these super big, super colorful trading card stickers starring your favorite superhero, Batman. Collect them, display them, or trade them with your friends.

Directions:	Write your request on paper, and put it in an envelope. You must enclose a long self-addressed, stamped envelope and **$1.00.**
Write to:	Mr. Rainbows Department P-6 P.O. Box 387 Avalon, NJ 08202
Ask for:	Two Batman trading card stickers

Really Radical Reptiles

These stickers are a must for dinosaur lovers. You'll get six brightly colored puffy dinosaur stickers to add to your collection.

Directions:	Write your request on paper, and put it in an envelope. You must enclose **$1.00.**
Write to:	Lightning Enterprises P.O. Box 16121 West Palm Beach, FL 33416
Ask for:	Six puffy dinosaur stickers

Rainbow Connection

Brighten up your sticker collection with these colorful puffy stickers featuring rainbows, unicorns, doves, flowers, and more.

Directions:	Write your request on paper, and put it in an envelope. You must enclose **$1.00.**
Write to:	Lightning Enterprises P.O. Box 16121 West Palm Beach, FL 33416
Ask for:	Six puffy rainbow stickers

ALPHABET STICKERS

"A" is for Animal

These sticker sheets have little animals shaped like all the letters of the alphabet and the numbers 1–9. You can spell out your name, your address, or a message to a friend. They stick to almost any surface and are reusable—use them again and again! You'll get four sticker sheets with a total of 288 stickers.

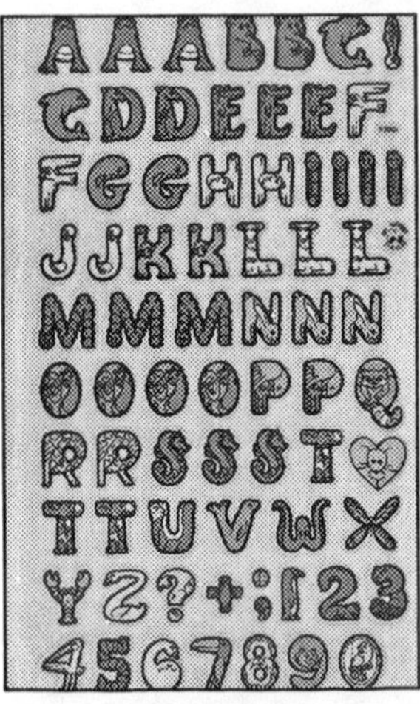

Directions:	Write your request on paper, and put it in an envelope. You must enclose a long self-addressed, stamped envelope and **$1.00.**
Write to:	Fax Marketing Department FS 460 Carrollton Drive Frederick, MD 21701-6357
Ask for:	Four animal alphabet sticker sheets

AMERICAN HISTORY AND GEOGRAPHY

Stars and Stripes

Tradition says that Betsy Ross designed the original American flag in 1776. But some sources disagree. Read all about Betsy Ross and other flag stories in this 7-page booklet from the Veterans of Foreign Wars of the U.S.

Directions:	Write your request on paper, and put it in an envelope. You must enclose a long self-addressed, stamped envelope.
Write to:	VFW National Headquarters Americanism Department 406 West 34th Street Kansas City, MO 64111
Ask for:	Ten Short Flag Stories booklet

Pledge Allegiance

Show your patriotism! Hang this 1½-by-1-foot replica of the American flag on your wall.

Directions:	Write your request on paper, and put it in an envelope. You must enclose a long self-addressed, stamped envelope and **25¢.**
Write to:	Meadowbrook Press Department AF 18318 Minnetonka Boulevard Deephaven, MN 55391
Ask for:	American flag

Father of Our Country

Did you know that George Washington never chopped down a cherry tree or wore a wig? Learn some facts about his life and presidency in a collection of brochures, booklets, and postcards. You'll also get excerpts from his boyhood journal, a brief biography, and a "scratch and learn" quiz card.

Directions:	Write your request on paper, and put it in an envelope. You must enclose **$1.00.**
Write to:	Mount Vernon Ladies' Association Education Department Mount Vernon, VA 22121
Ask for:	George Washington materials for kids

Our National Anthem

The Battle of Baltimore, during the War of 1812, was more than just an American victory—it sparked Francis Scott Key's writing of *The Star-Spangled Banner,* our national anthem. Send for these reading materials about the American flag and Fort McHenry to learn more. You'll also get a copy of the original *Star-Spangled Banner* song.

Directions:	Write your request on paper, and put it in an envelope. You must enclose **$1.00.**
Write to:	The Star-Spangled Banner Flag House 844 East Pratt Street Baltimore, MD 21202
Ask for:	Flag House materials for kids

A Piece of History

What did the Declaration of Independence really look like? How about the Bill of Rights? Send for these antiqued parchment replicas of historical documents, posters, bank notes, and maps. Each one goes through a secret 11-step process that makes it look and feel old!

Directions:	Write your request on paper, and put it in an envelope. You must enclose **$1.00** for **each** set you request.
Write to:	Historical Documents Company Department S 8 North Preston Street Philadelphia, PA 19104
Ask for:	Each set by name **and** number

Here is a list of historical posters, documents, maps, and bank notes to choose from:

- **#201S** Declaration of Independence and the Bill of Rights (enclose **$1.00**)
- **#202S** 14 Different Colonial and Revolutionary War bank notes (enclose **$1.00**)
- **#203S** 12 Different Confederate bank notes (enclose **$1.00**)
- **#204S** Map of the Voyages of Discovery and 1651 world map (enclose **$1.00**)
- **#205S** Pirate Treasure Map and Pirates' Creed of Ethics (enclose **$1.00**)
- **#206S** Jesse James and Billy the Kid reward posters (enclose **$1.00**)
- **#207S** Civil War map and Revolutionary War battlefields map (enclose **$1.00**)
- **#208S** History of Famous American Flags and Pictures of all U.S. Presidents (enclose **$1.00**)
- **#209S** Lincoln's Gettysburg Address and Lincoln's portrait and thoughts (enclose **$1.00**)
- **#2011S** The 1776 Continental dollar coin and 1778 $20 U.S. Continental bank note (enclose **$1.00**)
- **#2012S** Constitution and Star-Spangled Banner (enclose **$1.00**)
- **#2013S** Butch Cassidy and the Sundance Kid (enclose **$1.00**)

Historic Gettysburg

Gettysburg, Pennsylvania, was the site of the most famous Civil War battle. Today the town remembers and honors that battle with more than 1,000 monuments and other attractions. This 56-page guide tells you all about the history of Gettysburg.

Directions:	Use a postcard.
Write to:	Gettysburg Travel Council Department 201 35 Carlisle Street Gettysburg, PA 17325
Ask for:	Gettysburg tourism booklet

History of Paper

Trace the history of paper in the United States using this large poster. You can also get some materials with information about paper's environmental impact, careers in the paper industry, and instructions for how to make your own paper. Specify which items you want.

Directions:	Use a postcard.
Write to:	American Paper Institute 260 Madison Avenue New York, NY 10016
Ask for:	· How Paper Came to America poster · What's So Special about Paper? booklet · Paper and Paper Manufacture booklet · How You Can Make Paper foldout

Fun on the Run

Use this fun booklet when you travel across the U.S.A. It has 31 pages and is filled with great games the whole family can play while traveling by car.

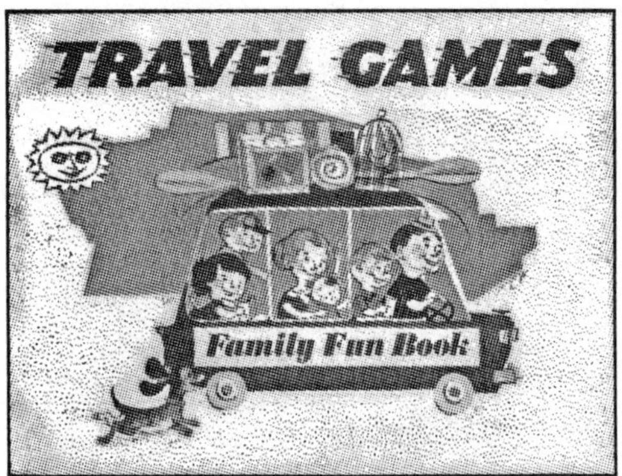

Directions:	Write your request on paper, and put it in an envelope. You must enclose **$1.50.** (*We think this offer is a good value for the money.*)
Write to:	The Beavers Department FS HCR 70, Box 537 Laporte, MN 56461
Ask for:	Travel Games booklet

Family on the Go

Car trips with your family are lots of fun—especially when you play travel games together! Send for this license plate game that features a U.S. map and a geography quiz. You'll also get a family travel guides catalog to make your next vacation extra special.

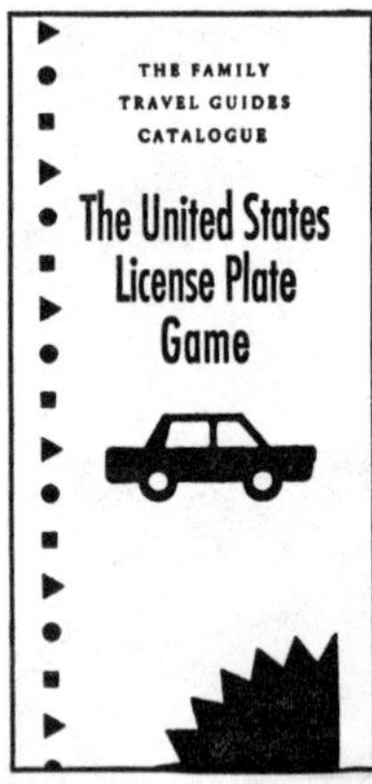

Directions:	Write your request on paper, and put it in an envelope. You must enclose **$1.00.**
Write to:	Carousel Press Family Travel Guides Game P.O. Box 6061 Albany, CA 94706-0061
Ask for:	U.S. License Plate Game and catalog

Be a Pen Pal

Make a friend in another part of the country without even leaving your house! A pen pal is a special friend you write letters to—you can exchange information about your state, neighborhood, school, and family with another kid your age who shares similar interests. The Dolphin Pen Pal Center will provide you with your new pen pal's address so you can start writing.

Directions:	Write your request on paper (*and include your age, grade, and favorite activities*), and put it in an envelope. You must enclose **$1.00.**
Write to:	Dolphin Pen Pal Center Department FSFK 32-B Shelter Cove Lane Hilton Head Island, SC 29928
Ask for:	U.S. pen pal

Take a Hike

Now you can have a colorful map of the United States that shows our 156 National Forests. Wherever you are, you're probably no more than a day's drive from a National Forest where you and your family can hike, fish, camp, or just sit back and enjoy the sights.

Directions:	Write your request on paper, and put it in an envelope. You must enclose **$1.00.**
Write to:	Consumer Information Center Department 136Y Pueblo, CO 81009
Ask for:	A Guide to Your National Forests pamphlet/map

America's Sites

The United States has a wealth of history and natural beauty. Now you can explore America's sites, parks, and monuments with these informative publications.

Directions:	Use a postcard.
Write to:	The tourism offices listed here
Ask for:	Tourism information

Booker T. Washington
Booker T. Washington National Monument
Route 3, Box 310
Hardy, VA 24101

Carlsbad Caverns
Carlsbad Caverns National Park
3225 National Parks Highway
Carlsbad, NM 88220

Custer's Last Stand
Custer Battlefield National Monument
P.O. Box 39
Crow Agency, MT 59022

Death Valley
Death Valley National Monument
Death Valley, CA 92328

Dinosaurs
Dinosaur National Monument
P.O. Box 210
Dinosaur, CO 81610

Edison National Historic Site
Main Steet and Lakeside Avenue
West Orange, NJ 07052

Frederick Douglass National Historic Site
1411 W Street SE
Washington, DC 20020

Fort Sumter
Fort Sumter National Monument
1214 Middle Street
Sullivan's Island, SC 29482

Grand Teton
Grand Teton National Park
P.O. Drawer 170
Moose, WY 83012

Ice Age
Ice Age Trail Project
700 Ray-O-Vac Drive, Suite 100
Madison, WI 53711

Lewis and Clark
Lewis and Clark National Historic Trail
700 Ray-O-Vac Drive, Suite 100
Madison, WI 53711

Lincoln Memorial
c/o National Park Service
NCP-Central
900 Ohio Drive, SW
Washington, DC 20242

Martin Luther King, Jr. National Historic Site
526 Auburn Avenue NE
Atlanta, GA 30312

Montezuma Castle
Montezuma Castle National Monument
P.O. Box 219
Camp Verde, AZ 86322

Monticello
Virginia State Chamber of Commerce
9 South Fifth Street
Richmond, VA 23219

Mount Rushmore
Mount Rushmore National Memorial
P.O. Box 268
Keystone, SD 57751-0268

Mount Vernon
Virginia State Chamber of Commerce
9 South Fifth Street
Richmond, VA 23219

National Cowboy Hall of Fame
1700 Northeast 63rd Street
Oklahoma City, OK 73111

Nez Perce
Nez Perce National Park
P.O. Box 93
Spalding, ID 83551

North Country
North Country
700 Ray-O-Vac Drive, Suite 100
Madison, WI 53711

Paul Revere
Paul Revere House
19 North Square
Boston, MA 02113

San Antonio
San Antonio Missions
National Historical Park
2202 Roosevelt Avenue
San Antonio, TX 78210-4919

Sunset Crater/Wupatki National Monuments
Route 3, Box 149
Flagstaff, AZ 86004

Thomas Jefferson Memorial
c/o National Park Service
NCP-Central
900 Ohio Drive, SW
Washington, DC 20242

Valley Forge
Valley Forge National Historic Park
P.O. Box 953
Valley Forge, PA 19481

Vietnam Veterans Memorial
c/o National Park Service
NCP-Central
900 Ohio Drive, SW
Washington, DC 20242

Washington Monument
c/o National Park Service
NCP-Central
900 Ohio Drive, SW
Washington, DC 20242

White House
President's Park
White House Liaison
1100 Ohio Drive, SW
Washington, DC 20242

Williamsburg
Director of Media Relations
Colonial Williamsburg Foundation
P.O. Box 1776
Williamsburg, VA 23187

Wisconsin Dells Visitor and Convention Bureau
701 Superior Street
Wisconsin Dells, WI 53965

Discover America

Whether you're planning a family trip or are just curious about your country, you'll want to send for these state and city tourism packets. Every state listed here will send something special.

Directions:	Use a postcard.
Write to:	The state offices listed here
Ask for:	Tourism information

Alabama

Alabama Bureau of Tourism & Travel
401 Adams Avenue
Montgomery, AL 36104

Greater Birmingham Convention & Visitors Center
2200 Ninth Avenue North
Birmingham, AL 35203

Mobile Convention & Visitors Corporation
1 St. Louis Centre, Suite 2002
Mobile, AL 36602

Alaska

Alaska Division of Tourism
P.O. Box 110801
Juneau, AK 99811-0801

Anchorage Convention & Visitors Bureau
1600 A Street, Suite 200
Anchorage, AK 99501

Arizona

Arizona Office of Tourism
1100 West Washington
Phoenix, AZ 85007

Phoenix and Valley of the Sun Convention & Visitors Bureau
1 Arizona Plaza
400 East Van Buren, Suite 600
Phoenix, AZ 85004-2290

Arkansas

Tourism Division
Arkansas Department of Parks & Tourism
One Capitol Mall
Little Rock, AR 72201

Greater Little Rock Chamber of Commerce
One Spring Building
Little Rock, AR 72201

California

California Office of Tourism
801 K Street, Suite 1600
Sacramento, CA 95814

Los Angeles Convention & Visitors Bureau
515 South Figueroa Street, 11th Floor
Los Angeles, CA 90071

San Diego Convention & Visitors Bureau
11 Horton Plaza
San Diego, CA 92101
Attention: Visitor Inquiry Mail

San Francisco Convention & Visitors Bureau
201 3rd Street, Suite 900
San Francisco, CA 94103-3185

Colorado

Colorado Tourism Board
1625 Broadway, Suite 1700
Denver, CO 80202

Connecticut

Department of Economic Development
Tourism Division
865 Brook Street
Rocky Hill, CT 06067-3405

Delaware

Delaware Tourism Office
99 Kings Highway
P.O. Box 1401
Dover, DE 19903

District of Columbia

Washington Convention & Visitors Association
1212 New York Avenue NW, 6th Floor
Washington, DC 20005

Florida

Florida Tourism Office
Department of Commerce
107 West Gaines Street, Room 501D
Tallahassee, FL 32399-2000

Jacksonville Convention & Visitors Bureau
6 East Bay Street, Suite 200
Jacksonville, FL 32202

Greater Miami Convention & Visitors Bureau
701 Brickell Avenue, Suite 2700
Miami, FL 33131

Pinellas Suncoast Convention & Visitors Bureau
Florida Suncoast Dome
1 Stadium Drive, Suite A
St. Petersburg, FL 33705

Georgia

Georgia Department of Industry & Trade
Tourist Division
P.O. Box 1776
Atlanta, GA 30301

Atlanta Convention & Visitors Bureau
233 Peachtree Street, Suite 2000
Atlanta, GA 30303

Hawaii

Hawaii Visitors Bureau
2270 Kalakaua Avenue
Honolulu, HI 96815

Idaho

Idaho Department of Commerce
700 West State Street
Boise, ID 83720-2700

Illinois

Department of Commerce & Community Affairs
Bureau of Tourism
620 East Adams Street, Floor M1
Springfield, IL 62701

Illinois Tourist Information Center
310 South Michigan, Suite 108
Chicago, IL 60604

Indiana

Tourism Development
Department of Commerce
1 North Capitol
Indianapolis, IN 46204

Iowa

Division of Tourism
200 East Grand
Des Moines, IA 50309

Kansas

Kansas Travel & Tourism Division
Department of Commerce
400 SW 8th Street, 5th Floor
Topeka, KS 66603-3957

Kentucky

Tourism Cabinet
Capitol Plaza Tower
500 Mero Street
Frankfort, KY 40601

Convention & Visitors Bureau
400 South First Street
Louisville, KY 40202

Louisiana

Louisiana Office of Tourism
Inquiries Station
P.O. Box 94291
Baton Rouge, LA 70804-9291

Greater New Orleans Tourism & Convention Commission
1520 Sugar Bowl Drive
New Orleans, LA 70112

Maine

Department of Economic & Community Development
Office of Tourism
193 State Street
Augusta, ME 04333

Maryland

Office of Tourism
Department of Economic & Employment Development
217 East Redwood Street, 9th Floor
Baltimore, MD 21202

Baltimore Area Convention & Visitors Bureau
1 East Pratt Street
Plaza Level
Baltimore, MD 21202

Massachusetts

Massachusetts Travel & Tourism
100 Cambridge Street, 13th Floor
Boston, MA 02202

Greater Boston Convention & Visitors Bureau
Prudential Tower
P.O. Box 490, Suite 400
Boston, MA 02199

Michigan

Michigan Travel Bureau
P.O. Box 30226
Lansing, MI 48909

Metropolitan Detroit Convention & Visitors Bureau
100 Renaissance Center, Suite 1950
Detroit, MI 48243-1056

Flint Convention & Visitors Bureau
Northbank Center, Suite 101-A
400 North Saginaw
Flint, MI 48502

Minnesota

Minnesota Office of Tourism
375 Jackson Street, #250 Skyway
St. Paul, MN 55101

Greater Minneapolis Convention & Visitors Association
1219 Marquette Avenue South
Minneapolis, MN 55403

St. Paul Convention & Visitors Bureau
101 Norwest Center
55 East Fifth Street
St. Paul, MN 55101-1713

Mississippi

Mississippi Division of Tourism
P.O. Box 849
Jackson, MS 39205-0849

Natchez Convention & Visitors Commission
P.O. Box 1485
Natchez, MS 39121

Missouri

Missouri Division of Tourism
P.O. Box 1055
Jefferson City, MO 65102

Convention & Visitors Bureau of Greater Kansas City
City Center Square
1100 Main, Suite 2550
Kansas City, MO 64105

Convention & Visitors Bureau of Greater St. Louis
10 South Broadway, Suite 1000
St. Louis, MO 63102

Montana

Montana Department of Commerce
Travel Promotion
1424 Ninth Avenue
Helena, MT 59620

Nebraska

Nebraska Department of Economic Development
Travel & Tourism Division
301 Centennial Mall South
P.O. Box 94666
Lincoln, NE 68509

Omaha Convention & Visitors Bureau
1819 Farnam, Suite 1200
Omaha, NE 68183

Nevada

Nevada Commision of Tourism
5151 South Carson Street
Carson City, NV 89710

Las Vegas Convention & Visitors Authority
3150 Paradise Road
Las Vegas, NV 89109

New Jersey

New Jersey Division of Tourism
P.O. Box CN 826
Trenton, NJ 08625

Atlantic City Convention & Visitors Bureau
2314 Pacific Avenue
Atlantic City, NJ 08401

New Mexico

Tourism & Travel Division
Economic Development & Tourism Department
Lamy Building
491 Old Santa Fe Trail
Santa Fe, NM 87503

New York

New York State Department of Economics
Division of Tourism
1515 Broadway, 51st Floor
New York, NY 10036

New York Convention & Visitors Bureau
Two Columbus Circle
New York, NY 10019

North Carolina

North Carolina Department of Commerce
Travel & Tourism Division
430 North Salisbury Street
Raleigh, NC 27603

Charlotte Convention & Visitors Bureau
229 North Church Street
Charlotte, NC 28202

North Dakota

North Dakota Travel Department
Liberty Memorial Building
604 East Boulevard
Bismarck, ND 58505

Ohio

Ohio Office of Travel & Tourism
77 South High Street, 29th Floor
Columbus, OH 43266

Greater Cincinnati Convention & Visitors Bureau
300 West Sixth Street
Cincinnati, OH 45202

Greater Columbus Convention & Visitors Bureau
1 Columbus Building
10 West Broad Street, Suite 1300
Columbus, OH 43215

Convention & Visitors Bureau of Cleveland
3100 Tower City Center, Suite 31
Cleveland, OH 44113

Oklahoma

Oklahoma Tourism & Recreation Department
500 Will Rogers Building
Oklahoma City, OK 73105-4492

Oregon

Oregon Tourism Division
775 Summer Street NE
Salem, OR 97310

Portland/Oregon Visitors Association
26 SW Salmon Street
Portland, OR 97204-3299

Pennsylvania

Pennsylvania Department of Commerce
Bureau of Travel Development
453 Forum Building
Harrisburg, PA 17120

Philadelphia Convention & Visitors Bureau
1525 John F. Kennedy Boulevard
Philadelphia, PA 19102

Greater Pittsburgh Convention & Visitors Bureau
4 Gateway Center, Suite 514
Pittsburgh, PA 15222

Rhode Island

Rhode Island Department of Economic Development
Tourist Promotion Division
Seven Jackson Walkway
Providence, RI 02903

South Carolina

South Carolina Department of Parks, Recreation, & Tourism
Division of Tourism
1205 Pendleton Street
Columbia, SC 29201

South Dakota

South Dakota Department of Tourism
711 East Wells Avenue
Pierre, SD 57501-3369

Tennessee

Tennessee Tourist Development
P.O. Box 23170
Nashville, TN 37202

Knoxville Convention & Visitors Bureau
P.O. Box 15012
Knoxville, TN 37901

Memphis Convention & Visitors Bureau
50 North Front Street, Suite 450
Memphis, TN 38103

Nashville Chamber of Commerce
161 Fourth Avenue North
Nashville, TN 37219

Texas

Texas Department of Commerce
Tourism Division
P.O. Box 12728
Austin, TX 78711

Dallas Convention & Visitors Bureau
1201 Elm Street, Suite 2000
Dallas, TX 75270

Fort Worth Convention & Visitors Bureau
100 East Fifteenth Street, Suite 400
Fort Worth, TX 76102

Utah

Utah Travel Council
Council Hall, Capitol Hill
Salt Lake City, UT 84114

Salt Lake Convention & Visitors Bureau
180 South West Temple
Salt Lake City, UT 84101-1493

Vermont

Vermont Travel Division
134 State Street
Montpelier, VT 05602

TOURISM

Virginia

Virginia Division of Tourism
1021 East Cary
Richmond, VA 23219

Norfolk Convention & Visitors Bureau
236 East Plume Street
Norfolk, VA 23510

Washington

Department of Trade & Economic Development
Tourism Development Division
P.O. Box 42500
Olympia, WA 98504-2500

Seattle-King County Convention & Visitors Bureau
520 Pike Street, Suite 1300
Seattle, WA 98101

West Virginia

West Virginia Office of Economic & Community Development
Travel Development Division
2101 Washington Street East, Building 17
Charleston, WV 25305

Wisconsin

Wisconsin Tourism
P.O. Box 7970
Madison, WI 53707

Greater Milwaukee Convention & Visitors Bureau
510 West Kilbourn
Milwaukee, WI 53203

Wyoming

Wyoming Travel Commission
I-25 at College Drive
Cheyenne, WY 82002

Casper Area Chamber of Commerce
500 North Center
Casper, WY 82601

ACTIVITIES

Neat Ideas!

Make cool toys out of things that you have around the house with these idea sheets.

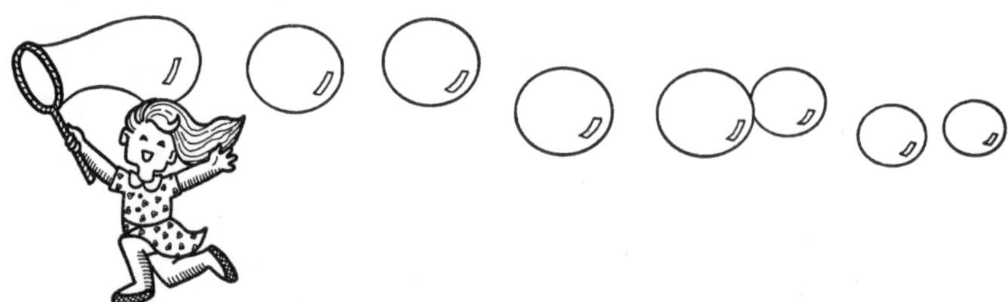

Directions:	Write your request on paper, and put it in an envelope. You must enclose **50¢** for **each** sheet you request.
Write to:	Children's Museum Shop 300 Congress Street Boston, MA 02210 Attention: Idea Sheets
Ask for:	• Balloon and Funnel Pump idea sheet (enclose **50¢**) • Tin Can Pump idea sheet (enclose **50¢**) • Making Large Bubbles idea sheet (enclose **50¢**) • Special Bubble Machine idea sheet (enclose **50¢**) • Pie Plate Water Wheel idea sheet (enclose **50¢**) • Raceways: Experiments with Marbles and Tracks idea sheet (enclose **50¢**) • Spinning Top That Writes idea sheet (enclose **50¢**) • Building Blocks from Milk Cartons idea sheet (enclose **50¢**) • Siphon Bottles idea sheet (enclose **50¢**) • Explorations with Food Coloring idea sheet (enclose **50¢**) • Stained Glass Cookies idea sheet (enclose **50¢**) • Making Simple Books idea sheet (enclose **50¢**) • Organdy Screening idea sheet (enclose **50¢**)

Makin' Raisins

Raisins are grapes that are dried out in the sun—they're a naturally sweet and healthy treat. This foldout and poster for younger kids features a fun coloring page and some easy recipes to try out at home.

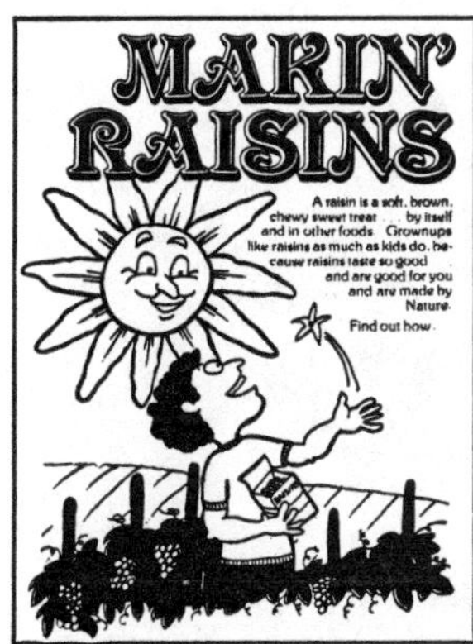

Directions:	Use a postcard.
Write to:	California Raisin Advisory Board Free Stuff P.O. Box 5335 Fresno, CA 93755
Ask for:	Makin' Raisins foldout and kids' poster

"Play Clay" Day

Gloomy outside? It might be a "Play Clay" day! Have lots of fun with clay you make with baking soda and other common ingredients. This foldout shows you how to make jewelry, ornaments, and more.

Directions:	Write your request on paper, and put it in an envelope. You must enclose a long self-addressed, stamped envelope.
Write to:	Play Clay Church & Dwight P. O. Box 7648-FSFK Princeton, NJ 08543-7648
Ask for:	How to Make Play Clay activity foldout

Full of Surprises

If you love to do puzzles, mazes, or crosswords, you'll love *SURPRISES*. This exciting magazine is full of games and activities, jokes and riddles, arts and crafts ideas, and more.

Directions:	Write your request on paper, and put it in an envelope. You must enclose **$1.00.**
Write to:	Children's Surprises Samples Department 275 Market Street, Suite 521 Minneapolis, MN 55405
Ask for:	Sample copy of *SURPRISES* magazine

Let the Good Times Roll

This coloring and activity book features the fun-loving "Roller Kids." It has pages to color, word games, and other fun activities.

Directions:	Write your request on paper, and put it in an envelope. You must enclose **$1.00.**
Write to:	Roller Skating Associations P.O. Box 81846 Lincoln, NE 68501
Ask for:	Roller Kids coloring and activity book

Lotsa Lists

Balaclava, pixie, sallet—these words might sound strange, but they're real. And they're all things you wear on your head! These sample pages from the book *I Love Lists!* are filled with long lists of everything from animals to foreign currency. The pages include pictures and fun activities, too.

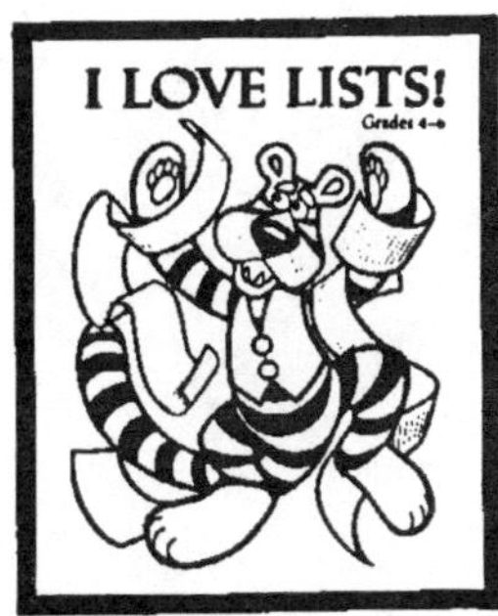

Directions:	Write your request on paper, and put it in an envelope. You must enclose a long self-addressed, stamped envelope and **50¢.**
Write to:	The Learning Works Department FSFK P.O. Box 6187 Santa Barbara, CA 93160
Ask for:	*I Love Lists!* sample pages

Think Ink

Get creative! This rubber stamp-making kit comes with six rubber stamps that you can make yourself. You'll get a heart, snowflake, teddy bear, cat, penguin, and flower to cut out, plus a simple instruction sheet and colorful catalog.

Directions:	Write your request on paper, and put it in an envelope. You must enclose **$1.00.**
Write to:	INKADINKADO Department FSK 76 South Street Boston, MA 02111
Ask for:	Fun stamp set

Watch Them Grow

Do you have a green thumb? Then try gardening! You and the sun can turn these seed packets, filled with hundreds of carrot and lettuce seeds, into a healthy salad.

Directions:	Write your request on paper, and put it in an envelope. You must enclose **$1.00.**
Write to:	Butterbrooke Farm 78-K Barry Road Oxford, CT 06478-1529
Ask for:	Special kids' salad garden seeds

Jolly Good Time

You can make a perfect popcorn ball without burning your fingers or getting them sticky. Send for this red plastic popcorn ball maker—it's a fun and tasty activity!

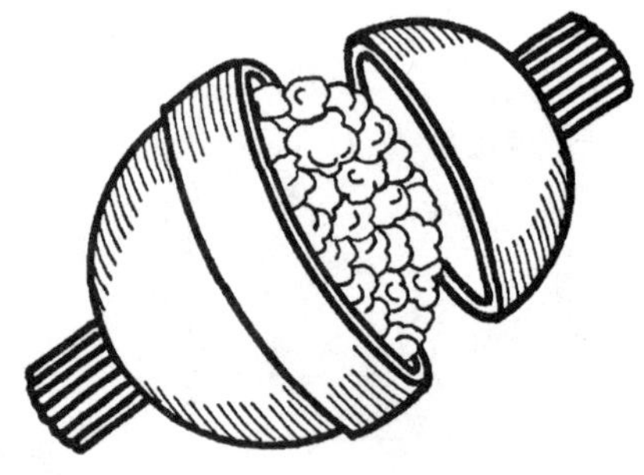

Directions:	Write your request on paper, and put it in an envelope. You must enclose **$1.00.**
Write to:	Jolly Time Pop Corn American Pop Corn Company P. O. Box 178, Department H Sioux City, IA 51102
Ask for:	Jolly Time Pop Corn Ball Maker

Count Your Stitches

This simple counted cross-stitch kit is perfect for beginners. It includes all the materials you need to make a colorful bookmark that says, "I Love Books," plus a simple instruction sheet. When you've completed your bookmark, take it to school to show your teacher or librarian.

Directions:	Write your request on paper, and put it in an envelope. You must enclose a long self-addressed, stamped envelope and **$1.00.**
Write to:	Adrienne Asnin Needle Nonsense 76 West Eckerson Road Spring Valley, NY 10977
Ask for:	I Love Books bookmark kit

Temporary Tattoos

Impress your friends with these colorful tattoos. You'll get a total of eighteen tattoos, including a Tyrannosaurus Rex, a dragon, and lots of little red hearts. They're easily removable with adhesive tape and can last for up to a week.

Directions:	Write your request on paper, and put it in an envelope. You must enclose a long self-addressed, stamped envelope and **$1.00.**
Write to:	Hey Kids, Free Stuff! 2022 Second Street, NW, #13 Washington, DC 20001-1634
Ask for:	Removable tattoos

Mini Mouse

Now you can have a mouse in your house. This craft kit contains all you need to create a cute and furry finger-puppet mouse. You'll get a set of mouse-making materials and an instruction sheet.

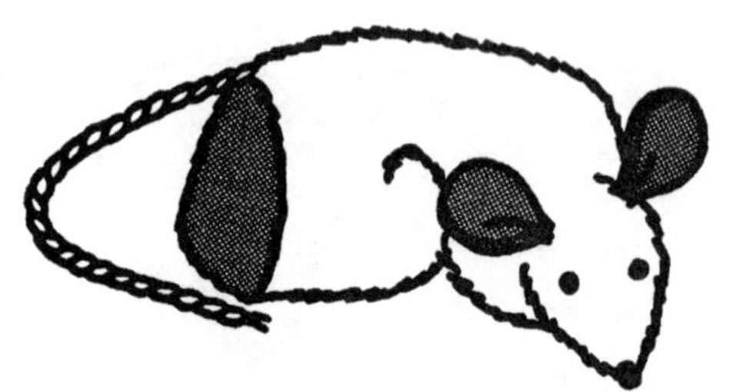

Directions:	Write your request on paper, and put it in an envelope. You must enclose **$1.00.**
Write to:	The Woolie Works—Mouse 6201 East Huffman Road Anchorage, AK 99516-2440
Ask for:	Finger Mouse craft kit

Clowning Around

Add a little fun to your clothes with these colorful clowns. Get a grown-up to help you iron on these velour transfers, and you'll have four crazy clowns dancing across your shirt, pants, or jean jacket!

Directions:	Write your request on paper, and put it in an envelope. You must enclose a long self-addressed, stamped envelope and **$1.00.**
Write to:	Pineapple Appeal Department FS P.O. Box 197 Owatonna, MN 55060
Ask for:	Clown iron on transfers

Make Your Move

Chess can be more than just a game with a friend. You can even play by mail! Send for this pamphlet to find out how to get involved in the world of chess.

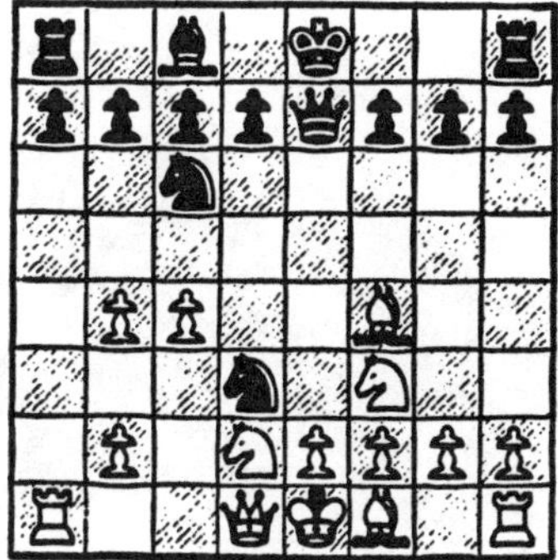

Directions:	Write your request on paper, and put it in an envelope. You must enclose a long self-addressed, stamped envelope.
Write to:	Barbara A. DeMaro U.S. Chess Federation 186 Route 9W New Windsor, NY 12553
Ask for:	Get Moving! pamphlet

Checkmate

Chess has a long, rich history. Most historians believe it was invented about 1,300 years ago in India. Today the game continues to fascinate anyone who enjoys a challenge. This 16-page booklet gives tips on winning strategies.

Directions:	Write your request on paper, and put it in an envelope. You must enclose a long self-addressed, stamped envelope.
Write to:	Barbara A. DeMaro U.S. Chess Federation 186 Route 9W New Windsor, NY 12553
Ask for:	Ten Tips to Winning Chess booklet

Scratch and Win

"Dr. Scratchov"™ has created some awesome scratch-off games featuring comic book-like art and some really creepy characters! Each game pack contains three scratch-off games so you and a friend can play the best two out of three. Collect the games, and earn enough points for fun free items like a yo-yo, bike siren, or even a skateboard!

Directions:	Write your request on paper, and put it in an envelope. You must enclose **$1.00.**
Write to:	Decipher Department FSK P.O. Box 56 Norfolk, VA 23501-0056
Ask for:	Scratchees™ game pack

Raisin' a Ruckus

Those cool and crazy California Raisins want you to grow up healthy and strong. Send for these colorful poster-sized foldouts that feature two different board games and lots of fun exercise-oriented activities like "learning to dance like a California Raisin." You may request one or both items.

Directions:	Use a postcard.
Write to:	California Raisin Advisory Board Free Stuff P.O. Box 5335 Fresno, CA 93755
Ask for:	• The Great Raisin Family Fitness Caper foldout • California Raisin Trail to Good Health foldout

SAFETY AND HEALTH

Safety First

"SAFE KIDS are no accident!"® is the motto of the National SAFE KIDS Campaign. To be a safe kid, you need to stay away from danger and take precautions every day. These magazines are filled with fun games, experiments, songs, and activities that teach you to play it safe.

Directions:	Write your request on paper, and put it in an envelope. You must enclose **$1.00** for **each** item you request.
Write to:	National SAFE KIDS Campaign 111 Michigan Avenue, NW Washington, DC 20010-2970
Ask for:	• Traffic safety magazine for kids • Fire safety magazine for kids

Carry Your I.D.

Staying safe is important. This "child file" is a good way to keep a record of all your physical characteristics for easy identification, just in case you get hurt or lost. The file contains a place for your photo, helpful safety tips, and a fingerprint kit.

Directions:	Write your request on paper, and put it in an envelope. You must enclose a long self-addressed, stamped envelope and **$1.00.**
Write to:	Special Products Department FS 34 Romeyn Avenue Amsterdam, NY 12010
Ask for:	ChildFile

Play It Safe

Now you can learn to take good care of your bicycle and ride it safely. Pick up these and other safety and health habits from this pamphlet and two coloring books. You can choose any **two** items.

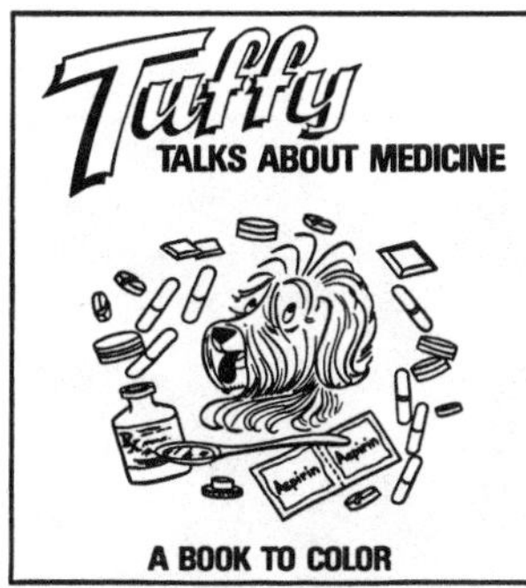

Directions:	Write your request on paper, and put it in an envelope. You must enclose a long self-addressed, stamped envelope for the pamphlet.
Write to:	Aetna Life & Casualty Corporate Communications DA/23 151 Farmington Avenue Hartford, CT 06156
Ask for:	· Safe Biking pamphlet · Play It Safe coloring book · Tuffy Talks about Medicine coloring book

Be a Safe Biker

This coloring book teaches you about bike safety and why these measures are important. You'll learn everything from hand signals to how to check your bike for safety before you ride.

Directions:	Use a postcard.
Write to:	Sandoz–Triaminic Route 10 East Hanover, NJ 07936
Ask for:	Helping with Bike Safety coloring book

Use Your Head

It's smart to wear a helmet when you're biking because you could fall off your bike and hit your head. Helmets protect your brain from injury—that's why football players, race car drivers, and construction workers wear them! This poster is a great safety reminder.

Directions:	Write your request on paper, and put it in an envelope. You must enclose **$1.00.**
Write to:	National SAFE KIDS Campaign 111 Michigan Avenue, NW Washington, DC 20010-2970
Ask for:	Helmet poster

Join the Bucket Brigade

Glue this red, white, and blue label to a one-pound coffee can to make an emergency fire pail. When you fill the can with baking soda, it's ready to put out any electrical or grease fire. You'll also get instructions and a fire chart.

Directions:	Write your request on paper, and put it in an envelope. You must enclose a long self-addressed, stamped envelope.
Write to:	Fire Pail Church & Dwight P.O. Box 7648-FSFK Princeton, NJ 08543-7648
Ask for:	Fire Pail label

Take a Deep Breath

You might know that you need your lungs to breathe, but what else do you know about them? The American Lung Association makes learning fun with a coloring book, a crossword puzzle book, and an activity book. Specify which items you want.

Directions:	Use a postcard.
Write to:	American Lung Association GPO Box #596-RB New York, NY 10116-0596
Ask for:	• **#0840** No Smoking, Lungs at Work activity book • **#0071** Let's Solve the Smokeword puzzle book • **#0043** No Smoking coloring book

No Smoking!

Tell your family and friends that you don't want them to smoke by hanging up this sign that warns: Lungs at Work No Smoking.

Directions:	Use a postcard.
Write to:	American Lung Association GPO Box #596-RB New York, NY 10116-0596
Ask for:	• **#0121** Lungs at Work sign

Smoking Isn't Cool

This colorful, full-of-action comic book stars the amazing Spider-Man and other superheroes who battle the villain, Smokescreen. Read it, and see how smoking affects your health and life—for the worse.

Directions:	Use a postcard.
Write to:	Your local American Cancer Society office. It's listed in the telephone book.
Ask for:	Spider-Man comic book

Dealing with Cancer

If someone in your family has cancer, you'll want to read these booklets from the American Cancer Society. They explain what cancer is, different treatments for helping patients, and how to understand the confusing thoughts and feelings you're having. You may order one or both items.

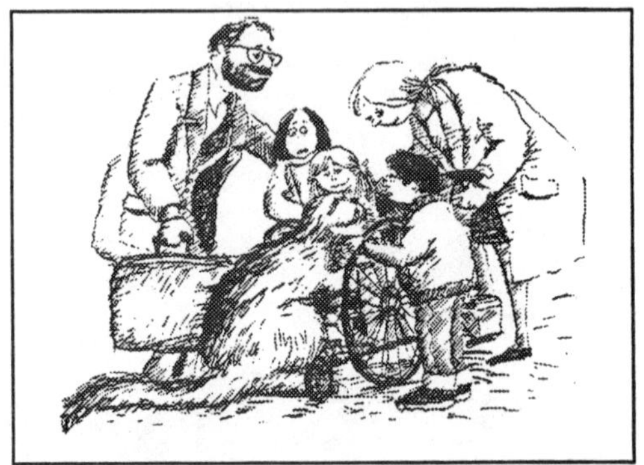

Directions:	Use a postcard.
Write to:	Your local American Cancer Society office. It's listed in the telephone book.
Ask for:	· When Your Brother or Sister Has Cancer booklet · When Mom or Dad Has Cancer booklet

Helping Hands

Does someone you love have Alzheimer's disease? This coloring book shows you what happens when a person gets this disease and ways for loved ones to help.

Directions:	Use a postcard.
Write to:	Sandoz—Triaminic Route 10 East Hanover, NJ 07936
Ask for:	Helping Grandma coloring book

Helping Each Other

This coloring book teaches you about four serious illnesses that sometimes affect kids and adults. You'll learn about diabetes, epilepsy, mental illness, and hypertension.

Directions:	Use a postcard.
Write to:	Sandoz—Triaminic Route 10 East Hanover, NJ 07936
Ask for:	Helping Each Other coloring book

Get Healthy

These colorful cartoon sticker sheets show you what you need to do to be a healthy kid. They'll help you remember to eat right, avoid drugs, get lots of exercise, and more. You'll get two sheets.

Directions:	Write your request on paper, and put it in an envelope. You must enclose **$1.00.**
Write to:	Special Products Department FS 34 Romeyn Avenue Amsterdam, NY 12010
Ask for:	Healthy Kids sticker sheets

Speak Silently

You can talk without making a sound. It's no trick with sign language. Many speech- and hearing-impaired people learn how to communicate using the same manual alphabet you'll get on this card and button.

INTERPRETER CARD
MANUAL ALPHABET

A B C D

Directions:	Write your request on paper, and put it in an envelope. You must enclose a long self-addressed, stamped envelope and **$1.00.**
Write to:	Keep Quiet P.O. Box 361 Stanhope, NJ 07874
Ask for:	Manual alphabet card and button

Just Say No!

What should you do if a friend or stranger offers you drugs? Just say, "No!" and then tell someone you trust about it. This coloring and activity book teaches you about the bad drugs that you should stay away from and their effects on your health.

Directions:	Write your request on paper, and put it in an envelope. You must enclose **$1.00** and **one 29¢** stamp.
Write to:	Safe Child P.O. Box 40 1594 Brooklyn, NY 11240-1594
Ask for:	Be Smart Say No to Drugs coloring book

Snuff Is Bad Stuff

Smokeless tobacco, often called "snuff" or "chew," is bad news for kids and adults. It can cause mouth sores, cancer, and even high blood pressure. Learn how to avoid this harmful habit by reading this pamphlet that folds out into a cool poster to hang in your room.

Directions:	Use a postcard.
Write to:	Consumer Information Center Department 555Y Pueblo, CO 81009
Ask for:	Chew or Snuff pamphlet

Tin Grins Are In!

You can learn all about orthodontics and wearing braces from this newsletter and two pamphlets. You may request one or more items.

Directions:	Use a postcard.
Write to:	American Association of Orthodontists Department KD 401 North Lindbergh Boulevard St. Louis, MO 63141-7816
Ask for:	· Smile of Health newsletter · Facts about Orthodontics pamphlet · Career in Orthodontics pamphlet

Looking Good

How can baking soda keep you healthy? Use it instead of toothpaste, as a mouthwash, and much more. This pamphlet tells you all about baking-soda health care.

Directions:	Write your request on paper, and put it in an envelope. You must enclose a long self-addressed, stamped envelope.
Write to:	Looking Good Church & Dwight P.O. Box 7648-FSFK Princeton, NJ 08543-7648
Ask for:	Looking Good pamphlet

Food for Thought

Don't loaf around—read this fun booklet about bread-making instead! It takes you on an illustrated tour of a bread factory where they do everything from mixing the ingredients to bagging the loaf.

Directions:	Write your request on paper, and put it in an envelope. You must enclose **75¢.**
Write to:	American Institute of Baking Communications Department 1213 Bakers Way Manhattan, KS 66502
Ask for:	Bread in the Making booklet

Rice Is Nice

Learn how climate and terrain combine to produce top-quality rice in many U.S. states. Send for more facts about rice and a pamphlet of low-fat recipes. You may request one or more items.

Directions:	Write your request on paper, and put it in an envelope. You must enclose a long self-addressed, stamped envelope for **each** item you request.
Write to:	The Rice Council P.O. Box 740121 Houston, TX 77274
Ask for:	• Facts about U.S. Rice pamphlet • Light, Lean, and Low-Fat Recipes pamphlet • Teaching the Fun Way. . .with Rice! booklet

Emergency!

Do you know what to do if you're involved in an emergency? These 16-page coloring and activity books explain first aid, calling 911, and what it's like to go to the emergency room. They include mazes, dot-to-dots, and award certificates that show that you know what to do in a real emergency.

Directions:	Write your request on paper, and put it in an envelope. You must enclose **$1.00** and **one 29¢** stamp for **each** coloring book you request.
Write to:	Safe Child P.O. Box 40 1594 Brooklyn, NY 11240-1594
Ask for:	· A Visit to the Emergency Center coloring book · In an Emergency Dial 911 coloring book · Know Emergency First Aid coloring book

INDEX

INDEX

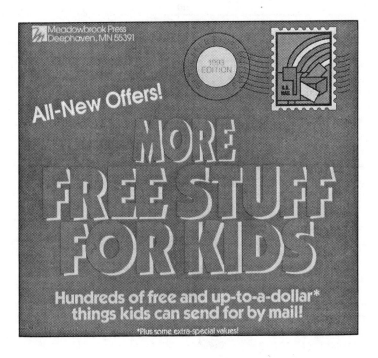

Order Form

Quantity	Title	Author	Order No.	Unit Cost	Total
	Almost Grown-Up	Patterson, Claire	2290	$4.95	
	Dads Say the Dumbest Things!	Lansky/Jones	4220	$6.00	
	Dino Dots	Dixon, Dougal	2250	$4.95	
	Free Stuff for Kids	Free Stuff Editors	2190	$5.00	
	Grandma Knows Best	McBride, Mary	4009	$5.00	
	Hocus Pocus Stir & Cook, Kitchen Science	Lewis, James	2380	$7.00	
	How to Embarrass Your Kids (Oct. '92)	Holleman/Sherins	4005	$6.00	
	Kids Pick the Funniest Poems	Lansky, Bruce	2410	$13.00	
	Learn While You Scrub, Science in the Tub	Lewis, James	2350	$7.00	
	Measure Pour & Mix, Kitchen Science Tricks	Lewis, James	2370	$7.00	
	Moms Say the Funniest Things!	Lansky, Bruce	4280	$6.00	
	More Free Stuff for Kids (Jan. '93)	Free Stuff Editors	2191	$5.00	
	Rub-a-Dub-Dub, Science in the Tub	Lewis, James	2270	$6.00	
	Sand Castles Step-by-Step	Wierenga/McDonald	2300	$6.95	
	Webster's Dictionary Game	Webster, Wilbur	6030	$5.95	
	Weird Wonders and Bizarre Blunders	Schreiber, Brad	4120	$4.95	
				Subtotal	
				Shipping and Handling (see below)	
				MN residents add 6.5% sales tax	
				Total	

YES, please send me the books indicated above. Add $1.50 shipping and handling for the first book and $.50 for each additional book. Add $2.00 to total for books shipped to Canada. Overseas postage will be billed. Allow up to 4 weeks for delivery. Send check or money order payable to Meadowbrook Press. No cash or C.O.D.'s, please. Prices subject to change without notice. **Quantity discounts available upon request.**

Send book(s) to:

Name ______________________ Phone ______________________

Address ______________________

City ______________________ State ____________ Zip ____________

Payment via:

☐ Check or money order payable to Meadowbrook Press. (No cash or C.O.D.'s, please.) Amount enclosed $____________

☐ Visa (for orders over $10.00 only) ☐ MasterCard (for orders over $10.00 only)

Account # ______________ Signature ______________ Exp. Date ________

A *FREE* Meadowbrook Press catalog is available upon request.

You can also phone us for orders of $10.00 or more at 1-800-338-2232.

Mail to: Meadowbrook, Inc., 18318 Minnetonka Blvd., Deephaven, MN 55391

(612) 473-5400 Toll-Free 1-800-338-2232 FAX (612) 475-0736